# COWBOY REDEMPTION

BARB HAN

TORJAKE PUBLISHING

*To my family for unwavering love and support. I can't imagine doing life with anyone else. I love you guys with all my heart.*

Reed McGannon had spent his entire life living and working on the ranch that had been in his family for multiple generations. Owned by his uncle now, Reed had grown up running around on this land, working this land, and loving this land as much as his brothers and cousins. It was as much a part of his soul as being Texan and he counted himself lucky to have been born into a career he would've chosen anyway.

Uncle Clive had raised Reed and his brothers after their father cashed in his inheritance and took off with the money. Never in a lifetime of working and living at the McGannon family ranch had Reed ever felt out of place, despite being Clive McGannon's nephew and not son. At least, not until now.

The air on the ranch had changed after Reed's father had returned broke and with his hand out. The chasm widened as he tried to worm his way back into his sons' lives. Then, the gap spread so wide he could run a herd through it when he was arrested for the attempted murder of his brother.

After being in a coma for weeks, Uncle Clive was finally awake. His memory was sketchy thanks to a blow to the head. And now he was returning to the place where it started in an attempt to jog his memory, the equipment room.

All four of Reed's brothers had come up with an excuse not to make this walk with their uncle, who might remember that their father—his brother—had something to do with the accident that left him in a coma for weeks on end. The very real fear he might not wake or that he might be a different person if and when he did, had hung heavy on everyone's minds. Reed had never been particularly close to his father. The man had cashed out his inheritance from the family ranch and then taken off while Reed was in grade school. It was his uncle who had stepped in to become that parental figure.

To say Reed had experienced mixed emotions in recent months was the understatement of the century. And the worst part? Reed had to know if his father was capable of such a revolting act. If so, did that same bad blood run through his veins like he feared it might?

Being a McGannon meant a lot in this town, in the state if he was being honest. No matter how much Clive McGannon made Reed and his brothers feel otherwise, they were and would always be the sons of the wrong branch of the family tree.

Sheriff Laney Justice walked in the front of the pack, alongside Uncle Clive. Levi and Reed were the two oldest and hierarchy was important in this family. They were still trying to figure out where a surprise son Kurt fit in because he was now technically the oldest. He seemed fine with letting Levi take the lead as he'd always done. In fact, Kurt owned his own business and didn't want anything to do with the ranch. He had to be convinced to build a home on the property so he and his daughter would be comfortable whenever they wanted to spend time there. That was the thing about being a McGannon. Once in the club, it came with all the benefits.

Kurt pretty much still had that deer in the headlights look, an outsider looking in, and now Reed knew exactly how that felt. His own father might have tried to kill Reed's uncle. How was that for a screwed-up gene pool?

Reed sucked in a breath as he walked side-by-side with his cousin and best friend since birth. Miss Penny and Hawk, second mother and ranch foreman respectively, brought up the rear. With every step toward the equipment room, Reed's heart beat in his chest a little faster. The metal tin of the equipment room roof glinted in the sunlight. It was early, getting cooler outside. Although, in Texas that meant high in the eighties, with a low in the sixties at night if they were lucky.

*Lucky.* Now there was a word. Reed had the kind of luck that had his now-returned father sitting in county lockup. And Reed resented him for it. The goodness inside him felt like it was getting more and more quashed. Like a campfire that was once roaring but was now down to embers and the occasional crackle.

He hated his old man. He hated him for walking out once he filled his pockets with family money. He hated him for disappearing and not showing up for ball practice or games. And he hated him for coming back, broke with a hand out for money and not a thought for the boys he'd left behind.

So, basically Reed wasn't exactly winning at life. Or maybe he was just mad at the world. Either way, his uncle— the man who'd been there for every bump and bruise of childhood, every raging hormone moment of high school, and was still there for Reed to this day—was about to see if walking inside a building could convict or release Donny McGannon.

There were so many questions Reed wanted to ask his father but didn't. Like, why just show up and not step in to be a father? Granted, Reed and his brothers were grown men now. Time had passed. It was one of many reasons that Reed hadn't gone up to the jail to see his father yet. If he could call the man his father. Reed wouldn't be able to stand to see the pitiful look on Donny's face. It would haunt him. That wasn't the part of himself that he hated. He hated that piece of him that still loved his father. He hated that needy bit that caused him to care what happened. He hated the part that hoped like anything that his dad was innocent.

"Pretty sky today." Levi glanced around, clearly fishing for conversation. He'd stuffed his hands inside his pockets. Then, brought them back out a few seconds later. He'd looked everywhere but at Reed. And Reed hadn't done much better. Odd behavior for two people who'd been joined at the hip for decades.

"Sure is." Reed also hated how big of a wedge this drove in between him and his cousins. It was half the reason his brothers made excuses to take off after Clive's big announcement that he would return to the equipment room as the sheriff had suggested. Reed didn't blame them. They were dealing the best they knew how. For some, that meant keeping a routine. For others, that meant throwing themselves into hard labor. For Reed, he had to know. The sooner, the better. If his dad was guilty, Reed wanted to rip the Band-Aid off.

"There's rain in the forecast this weekend," Levi continued.

"Might be good fishing weather."

"Yep."

Miss Penny cleared her throat from behind them. "I can certainly feel rain in my knees. Might come sooner than the weekend."

"Maybe take some ibuprofen." She wouldn't, but that wouldn't stop him from mentioning it anyway, like he always had before their conversations became so stilted. Tension hung thickly in the air like heavy gray clouds.

"I might have an extra bottle in the bunkhouse," Hawk offered. He and Miss Penny seemed to be spending a lot more time around each other since Uncle Clive's accident; everyone was speculating whether or not they'd started up together.

"Don't go to any trouble, Hawk." The soft way she spoke to him had some ears burning. The way her cheeks flushed when he looked at her wasn't helping matters. No one would begrudge the two of them a relationship, so them trying to hide made it that much more interesting and entertaining. The cat was out of the bag on that one.

A knot formed in the pit of Reed's stomach as the group stopped at the door to the equipment room. Uncle Clive took in a deep breath, glanced at the sheriff, and then unlocked the door.

Reed and Levi walked in together, as did Hawk and Miss Penny. Uncle Clive brought his hands to his hips. He took a couple of steps to the left. Then, to the right. He compressed his lips like he did when he was frustrated or couldn't find a solution to a problem.

"Do you remember where you were standing at the time of the incident?" Sheriff Justice asked.

Uncle Clive's forehead creased with concern lines. Based on his actions so far, he didn't want his brother to be guilty any more than Reed or the others. If anything, he'd been protective of his younger sibling in a way that Reed could admire. His uncle looked to be concentrating hard, the weight of the situation weighing heavily on him. Reed had no idea how his cousins felt or how their relationships would change if his father was guilty.

His uncle walked over to the row of tractors. He moved halfway up the aisle before he came back. He put his right index finger to his lips and moved to the next aisle. He made a couple of mumbling sounds before returning to the tractors. He disappeared down the aisle, so everyone followed. On the north end, he stopped and examined a tire. Then, he took two steps back. He pursed his lips together and started nodding his head.

"I believe I was right here, working on this tractor." He studied the concrete where he was convinced that he'd been. "An argument? Heated words?" His forehead wrinkled with concentration. "I can't be certain when it happened, but I remember having words with my brother around this spot."

A look exchanged between Levi and the sheriff. One that said Uncle Clive had just failed the test.

"Okay," the sheriff said quietly. "Do you remember what the argument was about?"

Uncle Clive shook his head and quickly added, "It's probably nothing. We butted heads all the time."

Reed exhaled slowly. He brought his hand up, stabbing his fingers into his hair. Uncle Clive was trying to help but he was digging a bigger grave for Reed's father. The sheriff couldn't tell them what evidence she had on his father. Meanwhile, his dad was locked up and had been for weeks. No bail was set, and it didn't look like he was coming home anytime soon. The worst part was that Reed couldn't say for certain that his father wouldn't let his ambition take over his good judgment. As much as it hurt to think that way, he couldn't help it.

Air. He needed air about now. And it was about time he visited his father in jail to ask him what really happened. Maybe, his father would lie. Maybe, he wouldn't. Reed had no idea either way, but he wanted to look the man in the eyes and decide for himself if he was lying. Not today, though. Reed wasn't ready. He needed to come up with a plan first—a plan for how to handle it if his father was guilty as sin.

"I have to get out of here," Reed said to Levi before turning to walk out the door.

Levi grabbed his arm.

"Hey, don't leave like this."

"There's something I have to do."

CAN *you ever really go home?* The question sat heavy on Addison Lowery's mind and in her heart as she navigated the roads back toward Cattle Cove, Texas, and the house that had felt more like home than her parents' place in Dallas ever had.

Radio booming, Addison gripped the steering wheel a little tighter as she took the highway exit that would lead her straight to her aunt and uncle's house. She hadn't planned on returning to this place and especially not so fast. She had put this town in the rearview a long time ago and had no plans to return. Except that cases were being turned upside down after the county coroner died a few months ago, and corruption with the former sheriff had been uncovered. She had questions. It had taken a while for the news to reach her and now all she could think about was her cousin's disappearance that had been ruled a runaway.

Summers in the small tightknit ranching community had been some of the best times in her life. Her parents owned a business in Dallas and worked long hours and she'd spent most of her childhood sitting in front of a TV with a frozen dinner and her homework.

So the end of the year had been her favorite. Or, she should say, those early days in June. The spring rains finally died down, the days were long, and the sky at night seemed endless.

Her aunt and uncle cooked fresh meals from vegetables that came from their garden. All four of them sat around the dinner table and her uncle told the best stories.

Ivy, her cousin, was six months older and Addison's best friend for most of her childhood. By sixteen, the two had gone off in different directions. Addison's father had a widowmaker heart attack and her mother didn't want Addison to go away for the summer anymore. Said going home alone to an empty house made her too sad. Addison had to pick up shifts at the deli to cover for her mom, so her mom could cover for the work her dad used to do.

Despite having a phone and a computer at home, Addison lost touch with her cousin not long after she stopped coming to Cattle Cove. The hours at the deli were long and Addison's mom needed company. So she stopped many parts of her life until recently when her mother finally met someone and remarried.

Too many years had passed without much contact. Ivy and Addison grew apart. Probably to be expected in teenage years and beyond. And then the call came asking if Addison had seen or heard from her cousin. The answer had been now. Now, her aunt and uncle had passed away within hours of each other. One from illness, the other from grief. And she'd been given the task of coming home to clean out their old house. *This should be Ivy*, Addison thought. But it was like time stopped for her cousin and she fell off the face of the earth. No calls home to her parents. No communication with family. Ivy's social media pages were static. No new posts for years.

One explanation could be that she just moved on from posting on her old pages and forgot about them. People did it all the time. A new platform came along, and everyone hopped onto the bright, shiny new toy. Half the time, no one bothered to close out of the old one.

Too many years had passed. Driving on the once familiar country road, sadness settled in Addison's chest. The job ahead would be hard. She wasn't looking forward to going through her favorite aunt and uncle's personal belongings, deciding what to keep, what to sell, and what to throw away. All she knew for certain was that she wanted something to remember them by. A memento to remind her of all the amazing summers she'd spent in Cattle Cove and how wonderful they'd been to her, welcoming her like one of their own.

Tears pricked the backs of her eyes. A couple of deep breaths, in and out, and she shook off the melancholy. She turned up her music and started mouthing the words to one of her all-time favorite songs, *The Dance*.

Music had been such a part of her summers in Cattle Cove. Between her and Ivy listening to songs way past their bedtime in her cousin's bedroom—hairbrushes as micro-phones while jumping up and down on the bed, and dancing around the kitchen on Uncle Bridie's feet—there was always something playing. Aunt Kay had a wonderful singing voice and she was always humming or singing around the house. And they'd had an acre of land in a cul-de-sac neighborhood. A two-stall barn in the back that housed a mare and a pony named Rosie and Peter, respectively.

A slow smile crept across Addison's face. They played *rock, paper, scissors* to decide who got stuck with Peter. This home was also where she learned her lesson about ponies being biters. Oh, sure, they looked all cute like miniature horses but their temperaments couldn't have been more different. What Rosie lacked in speed, she made up for in gentleness. She did all right but no one would make the mistake of putting her on a racetrack.

A rogue tear slipped out and ran down her face. She turned down the music so she could concentrate while she navigated the last few turns. She'd been off the highway a solid half hour and the lanes had shrunk down to two. The road was windy and gravelly, so she had to slow her speed.

Addison didn't want to count how many years it had been since she'd been back. She was embarrassed to admit her life had become so busy she'd forgotten these beautiful people, if not the memories.

There should be a bridge coming up if memory served. It was small and covered a creek...maybe after this turn. Nope. Right, it was after the next turn. It was bright outside, the sun high in the sky. She'd been up since six-thirty in the morning and it was nearly noon. Her stomach growled, reminding her that she hadn't stopped to eat lunch. She'd wanted to put this trip off but a strong piece of her wanted to know if something at the house would tell her where her cousin went or what happened to her. She missed Ivy.

All Addison remembered, and her teenage years were mostly a blur of growth spurts and mood swings, was her aunt and uncle calling to see if Addison knew where Ivy had gone. The hope in Aunt Kay's voice and then the resignation during the call would echo in Addison's thoughts for the rest of her life.

Ivy never returned home. Never set foot in Cattle Cove again. She'd been classified as a runaway after disappearing in Austin. Guilt about losing touch with her cousin struck Addison as hard now as it did years ago.

The crazy part was that Addison figured her cousin would surface at some point. She and her mother were so busy running the deli that it had become easy to push those thoughts and worries aside. Addison had reached out to her cousin. She'd sent texts that were never returned, wondering what she'd done to make Ivy so mad she didn't respond even to her anymore.

The bridge. How many times had they walked across this bridge? More of those memories surfaced—memories that filled her heart with so much joy.

Addison drove across the small bridge, and then sped up around the next corner. She rolled down the windows and let the breeze whip her hair around, slapping her in the face. A laugh tickled the back of her throat.

And then she saw a flash of something dart across the road. She was going too fast to stop despite slamming her foot on the brake. Her head lurked forward as she heard a *thunk* and a *yelp* that would haunt her forever.

Had to be an animal.

The second the car came to a stop, she threw the gearshift in park and bolted out of the vehicle. The seatbelt locked, slamming into her chest. *Come on.* She had to wait an impatient few seconds before it would release despite hitting the button multiple times. Her foot tapped on the floorboard as she searched for a wounded animal.

Whatever she hit was big but not tall enough to be a

deer. No bears in this part of the country, at least not at this time of day. Right? Uncle Bridie used to warn her about coyotes, though.

Dangerous animal or not, she had to stop to see if she could help. There was no denying the fact she hit something large.

A truck came around the bend and immediately stopped as her seatbelt finally released its hold on her. She tripped as she exited her vehicle and rolled onto the pavement. All good despite the gravel she'd be picking out of her palms for the rest of the day.

And then she saw it. The large black animal curled up on its side. Its whimpers cracked her heart in two pieces. Was it pinned underneath her tire?

2

"Looks like you can use a hand." Reed dropped down in front of the black Labrador retriever curled up next to the vehicle.

"Yes. Thank you." The female driver wasn't someone he recognized and yet she seemed vaguely familiar. She couldn't be from around here. The leggy blonde wouldn't exactly go unnoticed. "He just darted across the road."

Reed dropped down beside the dog.

"You're okay," he soothed.

"Are you Reed McGannon?" the shocked voice asked.

He glanced up but still couldn't place why she seemed familiar. "Do I know you?" Most people knew his family and it wasn't always reciprocated.

"Addison Lowery," she supplied and he really drew a blank.

The Lab was in bad shape. He wasn't moving his left hindquarters and he had bite marks along his body. A fight? He'd most likely got on the bad side of a coyote or black bear. Reed fished his cell out of his pocket. "I'm guessing this is the first time you've seen this guy."

"Yes." She must've seen the bite marks when she added, "Oh, poor baby."

She leaned toward him and the Lab snapped at her. He was hurt, protecting himself. "You better keep your distance. If he wanted to hurt you, he would have."

"Right. Sorry." She didn't seem to have a very good handle on injured animals.

Working the ranch, Reed had grown up around all manner of beasts, including the domesticated variety. He knew them well enough to realize getting too close to a cornered or injured animal could have dire consequences. The image of foot-long needles for rabies shots came to mind, despite that not being the case anymore.

Reed put in a call to the local vet. "Derek, I have a Lab with bite marks who just ran in front of a car. Where should I bring him?"

"What's closer, the ranch or my office?" Derek asked.

"Ranch."

"Can you get him there safely?"

"I'll figure out a way." Reed thanked Derek and ended the call. "What did you say your name was?"

"Addison. You knew my cousin Ivy," she said.

"Oh. Right. Bridie and Kay's daughter."

"That's right. I think we spent a few summers visiting your family's ranch." She motioned toward the dog. "What can I do to help?"

Reed took off his flannel shirt and wrapped it around his forearm. The Lab was losing a lot of blood. He needed medical attention as soon as humanly possible. The ranch wasn't far. "Stand back, so you don't get in the way."

"You don't have to be a jerk." She said the words low and he probably wasn't meant to hear them.

Hell, he wasn't trying to give her a hard time.

"I just didn't want you to end up on the wrong side of those teeth. He's scared and has no idea if I'm friend or foe. His instincts will tell him foe because he's about to bleed out and is the most vulnerable he's ever been in his life. So, even a normally sweet-tempered dog could become aggressive. We just don't know what we're dealing with here."

"Oh." She backed away from them.

"Addison? Is that what you said your name was?" He thought she looked familiar and it was coming back to him now that she'd mentioned Ivy.

"Yes."

"You're welcome to stop by the ranch to check on him once I get him settled."

"Can I come now? I'm the one who did this to him." She looked at Reed with serious cobalt blue eyes. The breeze played with her wavy wheat-colored hair, whipping it around her heart-shaped face. "He's not wearing a collar and that makes me responsible for him."

"I could use some help once I get him in the truck." He glanced at her cute two-door sedan. "What's the biggest thing you've ever driven?"

A wave of panic washed over those gorgeous blues.

"You're looking at it." She nodded over her shoulder.

There was no way he was fitting into that small vehicle, especially with a wounded hundred-pound dog in his lap.

"How brave are you feeling today?" He winked at her, trying to lighten the mood. As it was, she looked rattled and anxious. Her reaction was understandable under the circumstances. She seemed like a decent person. Hitting an animal would shake any caring person up.

She took in a couple of deep breaths and pursed her lips before responding.

"Are we close?" she asked.

"Yes. I can talk you through it. There isn't much on this stretch of roadway to navigate around." He caught her gaze. "I know we don't know each other very well."

"No. We don't." There was a definite edge to her tone and he realized how abrupt he'd been with her earlier.

"So this question might come out of the blue." He intentionally lowered his voice and spoke in as calm a voice as he could. He needed to gain her cooperation.

"Okay. Shoot."

"Trust me?" He was asking her to go out on a limb. "Because this guy needs help and we can't sit around here and debate whether or not it's safe for you to get inside my vehicle."

"Right." She scraped her top teeth across her bottom lip. Sucked in another burst of air as she cocked her head to one side. "Let's do this."

"The engine is still running. I'll pick this guy up and move as fast as I can while you hop into the driver's seat."

"Let me park my car and grab my purse." She pushed up to standing. "I'll open the passenger door for you."

The wheat-haired beauty made quick work of moving her vehicle. She pulled way off the side of the road, parked, and then was to his passenger door in a flash.

"You're okay, boy. I just have to get you…"

Reed was losing his edge today. He had an emergency kit for just such an occasion with a shot of adrenaline loaded and ready to go. He jogged over to his truck, keeping an eye on the injured animal. He unlocked his metal toolbox before retrieving a backpack.

Jogging back to the weary dog, Reed primed the emergency needle and put his wrapped forearm toward the dog for something to bite. He figured the guy would snap at him at the very least.

Needle in, Reed was surprised when the dog didn't snap his teeth. He squirmed and looked around nervously but there had to be something seriously wrong for him to put up with what Reed had just done to him. That, or he was one of the best tempered dogs ever.

"I promise this is going to make you feel better. I'm not here to hurt you." The dog might not be able to understand the words, but animals picked up on tone and intention, especially dogs. This guy had been through serious trauma. Bite marks on his torso. One of his ears was torn. He might have dashed onto the roadway to get away from whatever was attacking him. "We'll get you fixed up. Find your owners." If he had any.

ADDISON WAITED BY THE TRUCK, listening as Reed's calm voice seemed to soothe the dog. Her heart was breaking at the fact she'd hit him. There wasn't anything she could have done differently to miss him. As it was, she'd swerved. He'd come out of nowhere. There wasn't enough time or road to miss him completely.

This seemed like a good time to remind herself that the situation could have been worse. And yet, she couldn't stop the overwhelming feeling that this wasn't the way she wanted to start the week of cleaning out her aunt and uncle's home. Like it was a bad omen.

At least Reed had some medicine on hand to help the poor animal. The timing of him being the one to drive on this road was lucky. Then again, his family's ranch wasn't too far. There weren't a ton of roads in this area. Nothing like what she was used to in Dallas. The probability she would run into *someone* and especially a McGannon was actually high.

"That should have given the medicine enough time to do the trick." Reed heaved the dog up in his arms and the Lab was compliant. The six-feet-five-inch man who was made of stacked muscle and the kind of good looks that would have women lining up for a minute of his time had a surprisingly soothing demeanor. Probably made women literally swoon. At the very least, the animal seemed to be responding, relaxing in Reed's arms despite weary eyes.

"Someone must be missing him." He was a beautiful animal, with a jet-black coat and the sweetest pair of brown eyes.

"Out here? You'd be surprised. This is where people come too many times to dump animals, thinking they'll find a home somewhere. Many, I suspect, end up in much worse condition than this guy. A domesticated dog isn't equipped to take on a wild animal that will see it as prey."

"That's awful." She didn't want to hear that. It literally made her heart hurt. She wished she could live in a bubble where everyone was kind to people and animals, especially animals. "Which way?"

He thumbed the way he came.

She climbed in the driver's seat and managed a decent U-turn, thinking *here goes nothing.*

"You're doing great," Reed said, and she appreciated the reassurance.

"This is easier to handle than I expected." She glanced over and saw blood on Reed's shirt and arms.

"It's a good truck," he agreed.

"He'll be all right, won't he?"

"We have the best vet in the county. He'll be able to bandage him up physically. It'll be up to him to handle the rest. He's been through a lot and he doesn't look more than a year old." Those words nearly gutted her.

"Poor baby." A surprising sob tried to tear from her throat. Where'd that come from and why now? The stress of losing two people she cared about? The guilt from not coming to visit them in all these years?

"What did you say you're doing in town?" Reed asked and she was thankful for the change in subject.

"My aunt and uncle passed away," she said.

"I'm sorry to hear. They were good people." There was so much warmth and compassion in his voice now. She wanted to lean into it. "I heard they moved into a facility last summer."

That was more than she'd known. The call about her relatives had come out of the blue. "I'm embarrassed to say I didn't know anything about their situation until last week."

"Mind if I ask why?"

"My immediate family circumstances changed, and the family deli kept me busy. I had to help my mom run the place." She wasn't lying but she didn't feel the need to fill a near-stranger in on her family's heartache. She did, however, think this might be a good time to pick his brain about Ivy. "Did you know my cousin very well?"

"Afraid not." He shook his head. "But I understand about families being complicated."

There was a story behind those words begging to be told. For a minute, she debated asking the follow up questions that immediately sprung to mind. But it wouldn't do any good to get to know him or anyone else local for that matter. She was in town for a specific purpose, cleaning out her family's possessions and getting the house ready for sale. None of which she wasn't looking forward to. The thought of being alone in a house that used to be filled with so much life was a heavy blanket wrapped around her shoulders.

His comment was a lead into her next question.

"How well did you know my cousin?" she asked.

"Not very. We weren't in the same grade at school and I pretty much worked the ranch when I wasn't playing sports. Didn't leave a whole lot of time for much else. I think she might have been around during the summer, but I honestly couldn't tell you much more than that." He pointed to a turnoff. "That's me."

"Wow. I forgot how impressive your family's ranch is." Turning onto the two-lane drive, they were met with a guard shack and a security gate. There must've been some type of device on the truck because the gate started opening as soon as they turned onto the drive. And then she realized that Reed had some kind of remote in his hand.

"You've been here?"

"A couple of times with Ivy." Massive oaks stood sentinel on either side of the two-lane driveway. To the left, an even bigger tree held a tire swing. To her right was just a massive front lawn with nothing but grass. Off to one side, there was a firepit with around a dozen Adirondack chairs circling it.

Next to a two-story stone building was a parking lot. It easily fit ten or eleven vehicles. The spots were large enough for any of those vehicles to be trucks and a couple of them were.

She counted two trucks, an SUV, and a sedan. She figured a smaller car like hers was probably not as useful on a cattle ranch.

"Then someone might remember her," he said. "We can ask around."

"I'm surprised you don't," she admitted.

"Why should I?"

"She used to have the biggest crush on you." Since years had passed and Ivy was nowhere to be found, it wasn't breaking a confidence to tell him.

"Really?" He made a hmph sound. "I had no idea."

Now, it was her turn to be surprised. "I thought the two of you started dating not long after my last summer in Cattle Cove."

"Not me. You must have me confused with one of my brothers or cousins."

Addison was absolutely certain it was Reed. "You know that thing you said about families?"

"Yeah, that they're complicated."

She was beginning to realize just how true that statement was. And she wondered what else Ivy lied about or covered up.

**3**

"Not sure if you remember, but the parking lot on the left of the big house is fine." Reed racked his brain trying to remember Addison. Came up empty. He had a baseline memory of her cousin, Ivy. A blurry image. But, honestly, there'd been so many friends coming through the ranch between his siblings and cousins it was hard to keep track. He had always been more of a loner and the least likely to be caught throwing or attending a social gathering.

He realized how bad that sounded. But he'd been into sports and was one of the shy kids around outsiders. When he was around anyone with the last name McGannon, different story. Plus, keeping up work at the ranch was enough to fill his days. He'd had a couple of girlfriends when he was young.

Reed had never been the kind of person who needed to be around others all the time. He liked being out on the land where he could breathe. Since his siblings and cousins had similar personalities, he'd never felt the need to explain himself.

The family played baseball on Sundays. There was Sunday supper, which was a big tradition. People showed up and hung out. That was the extent of it. He would have remembered Addison if he'd seen her.

"When you came to the ranch, were you with someone other than your cousin?" he asked.

"Yes. She was friends with Declan. I don't think it ever went anywhere but we used to hang out with him. I swear she told me that she started dating you, though."

"I know the name of every person I've dated. And I would remember if I'd seen you before." She had the kind of understated beauty that left a strong impression.

"It's been forever ago. I was in middle school and always had on hard rock T-shirts from the 80s."

There was a kid he remembered who looked like she wore her dad's clothes all the time. But *that* kid couldn't have grown up into this woman. Could she? "Did you always have on a pair of gray sweatpants? And wore clothes that looked six sizes too big?"

"Um, yeah. If you're talking about a girl who always had on a baseball cap, that was probably me." Her cheeks flamed as she pulled into a parking spot and damned if it didn't make her look even more beautiful.

"Well, no wonder I didn't recognize you. I never got a good look at your face." Or much of anything else, either. She hid behind baggy clothes and her cousin most of the time, if memory served.

"I was always petrified to talk to any of you guys."

"Were we really that scary?" Yes, he was caught off guard. Reed had always worked the land and never considered himself above anyone else. He was a regular guy with a few extra zeroes in his bank account.

"No. Not really. No. Not you specifically." She parked and

waved a hand around. "It's just all. It can be...overwhelming to someone not used to it. Plus, the fact everyone in your family looked like they just walked straight off a billboard advertising men's underwear." Her cheeks flamed again when she said that last part and he couldn't help but smile. "I just mean that you guys were all good looking and..." Her voice trailed off as a red blush crawled up her neck. "I'm pretty much digging a deeper hole here."

"Nah, you're fine." Compliments didn't exactly insult him.

The Lab had been calm for the entire ride. Reed was more than a little pleased with how everything was going so far. Animals picked up on people's emotions and Reed wanted to give the dog as much peace as possible under the circumstances. He seemed like a good boy. The fact he hadn't so much as tried to take a nip meant he had a laid-back demeanor. The dog was a sweetheart.

"He's shaking," Addison pointed out. The concern in her voice stirred something long dormant inside his chest.

Reed stroked the dog's neck. Whether he was shaking from fear or blood loss, Reed couldn't be certain. All he knew was if the dog had an owner, the person had some explaining to do. His gut instinct said the dog had been dumped out in the country to fend for itself. Anger ripped through him at the thought. It happened far too often and the people who did it should be strung up in the town's square.

The kind of people who dumped an animal weren't usually the sort who made a home in Cattle Cove, Texas.

From the corner of his eye, Reed saw Derek barreling down the path.

"We'll get him the help he needs." It was a promise he didn't take lightly.

"I appreciate everything you're doing and thank you for letting me tag along to your home. There's no way I'd be able to get anything done today without knowing what happened to this guy." The sincerity in her voice struck a chord in Reed.

"You're welcome." He figured he could take her back to her vehicle once the Lab was settled.

Derek pulled up next to them in his white van. Reed waved him over, figuring the less he moved the dog, the better. Derek could assess the dog on the spot and see what they were dealing with. Granted, more tests and x-rays would be needed. Reed second-guessed his decision to bring the dog home, except that he didn't want the animal waking up in a strange place, no matter how warm and wonderful Derek's office might be.

Reed opened the passenger door as Derek rounded the truck. He had on his lab coat and his stethoscope hung around his neck.

"What do we have here?" Derek asked, examining the Lab first with a visual once-over. He smoothed his hand down the Lab's back and then held his palm out for everyone to see. His hand was streaked with fresh blood.

"I didn't even see him. He just came out of nowhere. I hit my brakes too late and I heard a thump." The anguish in her voice caused Reed to reach over and touch her arm for comfort. Contact shot electrical impulses racing from his finger to his torso. There'd never been so much heat in one touch before and, not to brag, but he'd had physical contact with a few women. He'd never been the playboy type, but he dated.

He blinked a couple of times unsure of what had just happened.

"Okay. First off, he's awake and alert. Those are good

things. I'm guessing you dosed him with the emergency supplies you keep in your truck here." Derek was all business.

"Yes."

"Good. I won't give him anything else for a while." Derek made eye contact with Addison. "He's been in a fight with something. Possibly a coyote or a wolf. He's probably lucky to be alive. If you hadn't hit him, he might never have slowed down enough to be caught and get the help he needs."

She nodded and the tension lines scoring her forehead relaxed a little bit.

Derek felt around on the Lab's body. "He was taken care of at one point and not that long ago. No collar and the fact no one has called my office searching for a black Lab gives me the impression he was dumped intentionally."

More of that white-hot anger lit fires inside Reed, boiling his blood. What did people think happened when they dumped their dogs out in the country and took off? A magic dog fairy watched over it? Leaving a tame animal to fend for himself in the wild basically made him prey.

There were occasions when a dog strayed from its family on a hike and ended up lost. Those were heartbreaking and generally involved searches late into the night. Some covered multiple days and the owners pulled out all the stops to find their beloved pet.

Problem was, this guy didn't have a collar.

"Think he's chipped?" Reed asked anyway, mostly for Addison's benefit.

Derek smoothed his hand across the Lab's hip and the dog jerked his head up and yelped. "You're okay."

Not a good sign. He was going to need x-rays on that hip. Reed hated the idea of the Lab being alone at Derek's office no matter how much care and attention he would get from Derek and his staff.

"He needs to go in, doesn't he?" Reed asked.

Derek didn't immediately answer. He took off his stethoscope and listened to the dog's heartbeat. When he was finished, he said, "There's a lot going on with him."

"X-rays."

"Yes. And I'd like to admit him into my hospital. He needs IV fluids and a full workup." Derek made eye contact with Reed. "I'm sorry. I know you were hoping to keep him here."

"I'd like to be with him. How fast will he be able to come home?" Reed didn't want him thinking he'd been dumped twice. Labs were some of the most loyal dogs in his experience. The trauma of being alone in these conditions was just downright cruel.

"Depends on him. He's young. He has that working for him and that's a lot. These young guys tend to heal fast. I have to stabilize him first and figure out what we're looking at with that hip. I don't have to walk you through the process."

Reed was already shaking his head. The family ranch took on enough rescues for him to know the lingo and Derek didn't need to repeat it.

"So, basically, you have to take him in," Reed said.

"Can I go with him?" The wheat-haired beauty surprised him with the question.

ADDISON WASN'T TRYING to avoid the daunting work ahead, despite the fact she wasn't looking forward to it in any form or fashion. Her heart literally bled for the dog.

"I'm responsible for him—"

"Not financially," Reed interrupted. "Bill the ranch."

"Oh, no. I can definitely pay for whatever care he needs." She didn't want Reed footing the bill for something that happened partly due to her.

"We have an account set up to cover these situations for rescues." Reed's admission made her feel a little bit better. At least he wasn't going out of pocket. "The costs can easily get in the thousands of dollars."

Oh, wow. She had no idea. Now, she really was relieved he'd offered. She didn't have that kind of money lying around. Her relatives' will hadn't been sorted out yet so she couldn't use any money she received from her aunt and uncle's estate. To be fair, she had no idea what that would net, if anything. Wills were complicated and everything had to go through probate.

"Are you sure?" she asked despite not having the kinds of funds that might be needed for the Lab. She would find a way. She always did. It had been the same all her life. When the restaurant was losing business, she revamped the menu and customers returned. She even managed to get a few write-ups in the local paper to pull in more business. Don't even get her started on the number of fliers she'd put up in neighboring businesses or the social media presence she managed to keep the deli on peoples' minds. There was so much more to running a business these days than just creating a good product. That was the foundation. She did what she had to do, put in the work, and if she had to, she'd have done the same for this poor Labrador.

"Positive. Besides, he ran into you."

"Still. I feel responsible for him. If I hadn't been driving down that road at that exact moment…"

"Whatever was attacking him might have finished off the

job. You might have provided an escape route for him and spooked his predator."

Well, she really hadn't thought about it in those terms. Reed made a good point, though.

"I need him in my office," Derek said. "You're welcome to come along."

"Okay." Her car was still parked on the side of the road and she had no idea how she would get back to it if she caught a ride with the vet.

"Mind if I come along?" Reed asked. "I'm invested in this guy too."

He locked gazes with her.

"Not at all." She figured he had a right to monitor the Lab's progress considering his family was going to pay the vet bill. And there was something else tucked deep inside her that made her want him to come with her, a primal need that she'd tucked away a long time ago.

Wow. Had she really cut off all contact with the outside world after her father's death? Her life had changed so much. In many ways it felt like she'd stopped living. Everything had changed and her life was set on a different trajectory. She grew up, become a companion to her mother. She set aside her own needs. And now her mother was remarried and, for the first time in a long time, Addison felt a sense of freedom. Was it wrong? Did that make her a bad person?

Maybe.

But there'd been so many changes forced on her. She'd stepped up and done the right thing, but at what cost?

Being in Cattle Cove the summer before losing her father had been the last time she felt like a kid. She'd grown up real fast. Was that a bad thing? Maybe not. She became responsible for the restaurant and learned so much about running her own business. She'd also been thrust into an adult world, dealing with vendors and making schedules for their employees. She'd accompanied her mother on trips to the accountant, trying to learn everything she could about balance sheets and how to prepare for tax season. Believe her, she was no financial wizard.

"Okay." That one word spoken out loud by Reed brought a strange sense of calm over her.

Maybe it was the sense of comradery she hadn't felt since Ivy. And maybe it was the first time she felt connected to someone in a very long time. She could admit that she'd been going through the motions of life, so immersed in trying to keep her and her mother afloat with the business, and to be honest, her mother emotionally, that Addison thought of little else.

The thrill of excitement at the possibility of spending more time with Reed reminded her that she was still alive in there. Somewhere down deep. But it was there. Because she was the most responsible person she knew after losing her father. And she'd carried the emotional weight of being the one her emotional mother and family business counted on for so many years now she'd lost count.

"Should we follow you?" she asked Derek.

"That works." He glanced at Reed, who nodded.

"Let's get this guy taken care of then."

With that, the passenger door closed as she started the truck and waited for Derek, figuring she could easily follow him. Her nerves were on edge but there was something right about taking care of this sweet dog.

Addison backed the truck out of its spot and then followed Derek off the McGannon property.

"I wonder if he has owners out there looking for him somewhere or a family trying to find him," she said to Reed.

"The fact he isn't wearing a collar isn't a good sign, but it's possible. Derek didn't mention anyone calling his office. It's common for folks to give local vet offices a call if they get separated from their pet on a hike. This guy could have been surviving on his own in the woods for days or weeks on his own before you found him."

For reasons she couldn't explain, those words struck like a physical blow straight to her chest. Breathing hurt and the act of taking in air suddenly made her feel like a fish on land must.

Surprising hot tears pricked the backs of her eyes and she couldn't for the life of her figure out what it was about his declaration that made her feel exposed and vulnerable.

## 4

"Whatever happened to your cousin, by the way?" Reed asked. The accident seemed to have strung Addison's nerves tight. The way she white-knuckled the steering wheel said she was back on high alert. If he got her talking, maybe he could help her relax again.

"That's a good question and one I'm hoping to find the answer to while I'm here closing up my aunt and uncle's affairs." She shrugged and there was a lonely quality to her voice that he connected to on a base level.

"Again, I'm sorry for your loss. They were good people."

"Thank you, Reed. I mean it. Your kindness means so much. I loved my aunt and uncle dearly and wished like everything I'd come out to see them more." There was something about hearing his name roll off her tongue so easily, like they'd known each other forever, that stirred his chest again. "As far as my cousin goes, do you remember anything about the last time you saw her?"

"I wish I did. You said she knew Declan. I can shoot him

a text to see if he remembers anything once we get this guy settled." He motioned toward the dog on his lap.

"That would be nice if you don't mind."

"No problem," he said. It really wasn't. A text was easy enough to send and if it could help provide answers, he was happy to lend a hand.

Derek took a right, and then he pulled into the parking lot at his clinic. Addison followed and pulled in next to his spot.

A flurry happened next. Sonja, one of Derek's assistants, was waiting with a shorter gurney. As soon as the vet opened his door, activity started. Sonja came running toward them pushing the gurney. Derek opened the passenger door to the truck.

"Let's get him inside," Derek said.

The gurney was pushed up beside Reed as Derek helped ease the dog onto it. And then, the Lab looked over at Reed with the most pitiful eyes, like his security blanket had just been ripped out from underneath him.

"Hold on there, buddy. I'm coming." Reed was out the door and hightailing it inside the clinic in a heartbeat. He kept one hand on the dog's neck and one eye on Addison as she hurried alongside him. Her hand slipped inside his and he tried to ignore the hit to his heart that came with contact and the electrical impulses firing up his arm.

Reed had seen enough of the inside of medical facilities, be it clinics or hospitals, to last a lifetime after visiting the uncle who was more like a father during his recovery. And speaking of family, he wasn't looking forward to the trip he needed to make to see his father, the one to county lockup.

Pushing the thought aside, Reed stopped at the doorway to exam room one. He tightened his grip around Addison's hand as Derek turned to face them.

"Give me a few minutes to run some tests. You can wait in my office. The door will be open so you'll be able to see and hear everything as it happens." The door to exam room one was connected to Derek's private office.

Reed nodded, thinking the dog's eyes, his sad look, would haunt Reed for a long time. He led Addison into the adjacent office. There was a modern desk, light wood and metal legs, along with twin chairs on one side of the room. On the other was a sofa and a small kitchenette. Reed knew for certain that Derek had spent countless nights on the couch after a long day's work. His was a twenty-four-seven job at times. He was also the best in the county and probably the state.

"Do you want something to drink? Water? Coke?" Reed knew where the minifridge was located and the kinds of drinks Derek usually kept on hand.

"Coke would be nice." She took a seat on the couch, leaned forward and clasped her hands together. "I can't stop thinking about the poor guy in the next room."

"He's in the best possible place to get the help he needs to heal. He'll be looked after. Now, we can only hope for the best. Hope the guy's road to recovery is smooth." Reed pulled two cans from the fridge before joining her on the couch.

She nodded, taking one of the offerings after opening it. "What about his owners?"

"I'll be sure and ask Derek if anyone has reached out. Other than that, we can put up fliers and Miss Penny will know how to post in a neighborhood chat. I think she mentioned something about being in one with a few others."

She seemed satisfied with his answer.

He opened the cokes and fished his cell phone out. He

needed to get her mind on something else and he could admit to being mildly curious about what happened to her cousin. Until recently, there hadn't been much crime in Cattle Cove to speak of although the death of the county coroner exposed cover-ups by him, the sheriff, and the town's former mayor. "You said before that you're hoping to find out what happened to your cousin. I can text my cousin real fast, but do you mind telling me what you already know?"

"That's just it. I don't know much at all. I used to come here summers to spend with my cousin before my father passed away." Her voice hitched on the last couple of words, the pain still seemed raw. "Sorry. I don't talk about him much."

"We can change the subject if you'd like." He didn't want to add to her pain.

"No. I'm good. I need to talk about him. I never do. I've never wanted to before."

Words lacked, so he reached over and covered her hand in his, noticing how small it was by comparison and how soft her creamy skin felt.

"He died suddenly. Heart attack. He and my mother owned a deli and worked all the time. I was a latchkey kid and learned early on to take care of myself. Coming here in summers showed me a different way of life. My cousin's family ate dinner at the table together every night, whereas at home, I sat in front of the TV alone and did homework. Here, we danced. The three of us danced in the kitchen while my aunt sang. There was music and laughter everywhere here." She stopped like she needed a minute to gather herself before continuing. He squeezed her hand in a show of support.

"Sounds like great memories." Reed figured those were

all a person had in the end when they got too old to travel or too frail to work. Before his uncle's accident—and he was still calling it that because he needed it to be true—there was no way he thought anyone who worked at the ranch would ever be too frail. The accident had Reed rethinking a lot of things he thought he knew, especially the part about his own father being capable of hurting someone he cared about for his own financial gain.

"They are." She wiped away tears gathering in her eyes. "Sorry. It's hard to think of them as gone."

He nodded.

"They were so vibrant and I should have visited more often. I might have known when they were moving to a home. I might have been able to bring them half the joy in their later years as they brought me in mine growing up." She stopped long enough to take a sip of coke.

He knew all about the word *should*. The guilt that came with it. He should go to the jail and speak to his father. And yet he kept finding reasons to put off the trip.

"After my dad passed away, my mom kind of lost it. They were high school sweethearts and he was all she knew. They were so close that, at times, I felt like a third wheel." She paused long enough to take in a breath. "I was almost sixteen when it happened and had to step up to help with the deli or we'd lose everything, including a roof over our heads."

"Sounds like a difficult situation for someone who was grieving." Her courage at such a young age was impressive.

"Honestly, I had no time. Between the complete and utter shock of what happened and then jumping into the family business, I stuffed everything down deep and did my best to forget all about it."

"Why do strong people always do that? Think they have

to cover everything?" He'd been doing that for weeks. Ever since his uncle's accident. Reed had been keeping his feelings in check when he wanted to punch a hole in the wall. Granted, he wouldn't do that, but he sure as hell wanted to more times than he cared to count. He wanted something to release the pent-up energy.

And now?

He wanted the security of knowing that he would never turn out like his father despite the fact no one could guarantee it.

"I NEVER REALLY THOUGHT ABOUT it before," Addison admitted. "It's true, though. I'm generally the last person to show it when I'm hurting. I think seeing my mom fall apart like she did after losing my father made me think I had to be strong for her. Like she wouldn't make it...*we* wouldn't make it...if I didn't step up. It's strange now that I think about it, considering I was so young. She just seemed so...lost."

"It's a heavy burden to put on someone who was barely old enough to drive a car."

Addison exhaled. *Really* exhaled. It was the first time in so long that she didn't feel like she had to tiptoe around a hard topic. It was the first time she actually wanted to talk to someone about how devastating it had been to lose her father. And it was the first time she wanted someone to understand where she was coming from.

"Wow. When you put it like that, it gives me a whole new perspective." There was something about their connection, about her hand in his, that brought a sense of calm over her that allowed her to continue.

"Where is your mother now?"

"She's remarried. Can't say he's my favorite person ever but at least she has someone to talk to now. She was so devastated after losing my dad that she shut down. I did everything I could to keep her going. She eventually started waking up on her own and coming downstairs to eat after I made breakfast." Addison shrugged. "I can't say she ever seemed all that happy with my dad but losing him wrecked her."

"Love is one thing. Dependency is another."

"She and Dad were a team. I don't think she ever learned how to operate on her own, if that makes sense. I stepped in to fill his shoes in the business and, I guess, became her only friend in the process."

"And school?"

"I finished high school. Barely. Skipped my plans to go to college in favor of staying home to work and keep my dad's dream alive." She shrugged again. "Figured there wasn't much they could teach me at school that I didn't already know about running a deli and, again, Mom needed the emotional support after losing her person in the world. She would have collapsed if I'd left her alone."

He was nodding his head like he understood. She also noticed he compressed his lips like he was literally biting back what he truly wanted to say. "What about her husband now?"

"He's okay. She might not seem as happy but she's more settled. He was a butcher at the grocery store after he got into some trouble with the law. I think he was part of a second chance program for ex-cons who weren't violent criminals. My mom brought him into the deli after he chatted her up at the grocery. I wasn't all that keen on hiring him at first, but Mom met him through a social club that I pushed her into joining. I couldn't exactly criticize her choice after forcing her into the meet ups. Plus, I wanted to keep a closer eye on him. Get a feel for what kind of person he was."

"And? What did you decide?"

"I'm not a fan and there's just something about him that I don't fully trust. Could be that I would feel like that about anyone who isn't my dad, but this guy is definitely not my cup of tea. He seems to make Mom happy. Or at least happier," she admitted and this was the most she'd talked about her family to anyone. This was the most personal she'd gotten with anyone. Granted, she dated. There just hadn't been anyone who made her comfortable enough to really talk to. Maybe it was the extreme circumstances under which they'd bumped into each other or something else, something more primal, but talking to Reed felt like the most natural thing.

"Will your mother be joining you at some point?" he asked.

"No. My aunt and uncle left her out of the will. It's strange because I think she and her sister were close at one time. A long time ago. Once my parents opened the deli, which was basically my entire life, my folks dropped off the radar and the business became their world. My aunt never said a bad word about my mother behind her back, so I have no idea what happened between them or if anything did. They were pleasant to each other when they met in between Dallas and Cattle Cove to hand me off. I'd say in the last summer maybe less so. Nothing happened between them that stood out to me or caught my attention. If they were fighting, they hid it pretty well." Looking back, she should have noticed more. She'd been too caught up being a teenager, not wanting to go home and sulking when she did.

"I'm guessing your mother had no idea what happened to Ivy."

"None that she mentioned to me." Not that the two were close. "I remember the call from my aunt like it was yesterday, though. It came early in the morning. Before my parents went to work. We still had a landline for the security system. The phone almost never rang, especially not so early in the morning. I heard my mother in the hallway. When she mentioned Ivy's name, I came out of bed so I could hear what was going on."

Reed leaned toward her. His willingness to listen, to really hear her brought such a sense of calm over her. She knew better than to get used to it.

"My mom covered the receiver with one hand and asked if I'd heard from my cousin. I told her that I hadn't and then Aunt Kay must've asked to speak to me. I got on the line and told her everything I knew, which was basically nothing. We said our goodbyes and I thought nothing of it. I figured Ivy overslept at someone's house. It's funny all the optimistic excuses the brain makes up in these situations. My folks sat me down a couple of days later and said that Ivy ran away and that if she contacted me, I had to let them know right away. They asked for my phone passwords and searched around on my laptop." All Addison remembered clearly was how violated she felt having her parents go through her personal accounts. They read texts and social media posts. All embarrassing. And also convinced her that they didn't trust her.

"I remember being very protective of my phone at that age," he said. "Despite never doing anything illegal," he admitted.

"You feel like you have to hide something even though you don't," she agreed. "It felt like such an invasion that I pulled back even more from my parents after that. I didn't understand the gravity of what was going on. I thought Ivy took off for the weekend without telling anybody and would be back. You know?"

"It's too much for anyone to process, let alone a teen."

"My dad's widowmaker heart attack came six months later so it was easy to forget about my cousin. Ivy never did come back. No more posts on her social media accounts. I'm guessing at some point my aunt and uncle figured she was gone."

"Law enforcement doesn't spend a lot of resources tracking down runaways either," he said.

"Really? That's unfortunate. I was hoping to find something like a case file. Maybe figure out where she was last seen if that's possible. Right now, finding her is like searching for a needle in a haystack."

"I highly doubt you'll find a file here. The sheriff we used to have in Cattle Cove has been linked to cover-ups. He would have been sheriff during that time, and I don't think he would have been much help to your family."

She'd read recently about the coroner's death upending some cases in the area.

"No one ever found her and she never returned?" he asked.

"Nope. And it's strange because you have to try really hard these days to stay off social media. It's hard to hide," she pointed out.

"Unless you are very determined."

"Which makes me think she had no choice. I mean, maybe I'm being naïve, and I have no idea what her relationship with her parents became after the last summer I spend here, but it seems like she wouldn't want them to worry about her. She never came across as that selfish to me before. Summers with her parents were some of my happy childhood memories. They taught me what a close family looked like and I always felt like I belonged. I can't think of one good reason my cousin would shut them out of her life."

"Drugs. She might have gotten mixed up with the wrong crowd. Austin isn't too far from here and there's an underground music scene there beyond anything I've ever seen. She could have gotten mixed up with a guy who turned her against her parents. Controlling guys do that. Cut people off from their families. Isolate them. Minimize their world so they come to solely rely on one individual." His face twisted as he talked. He issued a sharp sigh. "Anyone who does that should be strung up by their..." He glanced up at her. "You know what I mean."

"Yes, I do." She paused for a few seconds. "It's possible she could've got mixed up into something. I just never wanted to believe it. When I really think about it, Ivy was quiet when she was around others. It was easy to forget because we were usually at her house, in her environment where she was chatty and outgoing. We rarely ever left the ranch, except to come to your place the few times we were invited. Seems like most of you were playing ball when we were there."

"Sunday afternoon baseball. Then you guys must have been a fan of my cousin, Ryan," he said with a devastating smile.

"I'm pretty sure my cousin was a fan of yours," she said matter of fact. It was true. She might have been friends with Declan but Reed was the one her cousin talked about constantly. "She wrote your name on her notebooks with a bunch of hearts. I remember that distinctly. They would be lying all over her room. Out in the open for anyone to see."

He shrugged. "I seriously had no idea. The age difference at the time could have been a factor. A few years difference can seem big in high school whereas, in your twenties or thirties, it's nothing."

"Funny how we can be so into something and yet keep it such a secret from the one person who deserved to know," she surmised. "I mean, you might have even believed she was together with your cousin and so never looked twice."

5

D erek poked his head into the office. "X-rays look good. The bite marks are troublesome, but I've managed to stop any bleeding and even got antibiotic ointment on him to help with surface wounds. I'm giving him IV antibiotics and I'll be sending you home with oral ones. His hip is tender but he'll be up and around shortly."

"That's good news." Reed had feared the worst when they brought the Lab in. Addison reached over and touched his arm. He ignored the jolt of electricity. "Have you gotten any calls about missing dogs?"

"None." Derek's gaze shifted to Addison and then back to Reed. "Will one of you be taking him home?"

"Yes," they both said at exactly the same time.

"I'll let you two work out the details." Derek chuckled. "He's a sweet one. Timid. Might make someone a good companion if they could gain his trust."

"What's your guess about his background, based on your experience? Is it a bad idea to get too attached to him? Do you think some little girl's heart is breaking as she's waiting for her puppy to come home?" Reed asked.

"I wouldn't want to be wrong about something as important as a little girl and her puppy. If this guy had a home anywhere in this town and the owners wanted him back, I probably would have heard something by now. That's not a hundred percent guarantee but it's as close as I can get to one." He twisted his face in frustration. "There's a good dog hiding behind all that fear."

"I'll have fliers made up. Give his owners a chance to step forward. If they don't have a good excuse for what happened to him, they don't deserve to keep him." Reed figured putting out a call would ease Addison's mind as well. If no one claimed him, the dog would get a new lease on life with Addison or him.

"What should we call him in the meantime?" Addison asked.

"Pup. Dog. Anything but a real name."

She shot him a surprised look.

"Once you give something a name, it's harder to let it go."

"Makes sense." There was a whole lot of disappointment in her voice that tightened the knot already forming in his gut. Letting her down, even in some small way, was the equivalent of kicking a puppy.

Detachment was a good thing. Being able to separate his emotions and put them in boxes kept his sanity after his father walked out on Reed and his younger brothers. The skill kept him grounded when his father walked back into his life, asking for a second chance at the ranch. And it kept him from losing it when his father was arrested for attempted murder.

Speaking of which, the sheriff was being tightlipped.

Reed wanted to know the evidence she had against his father. A trip to the county jail could clear up a whole lot of this mess. A dark thought struck. One he didn't want to let see light of day.

"I need to keep him for a couple of hours for the IV. Then, I can release him, if you don't want him spending the night here."

Addison caught Reed's gaze. The question in her eyes tightened more of that knot.

"Give us a minute, please," he said to Derek.

"Take all the time you need." Derek's lobby was never empty during open clinic hours.

Reed didn't want to crush the glimmer of hope in her eyes with reality. So, instead, he asked her opinion. "What do you think should happen here?"

"I don't know." She sucked in her bottom lip and then released it. He didn't want to notice the silky trail her tongue left when it retreated.

"Let me rephrase that." He decided to take another tact. "What would you like to happen?"

"Are we talking about a perfect world here?" she asked, her voice laced with anger.

"Sure. Why not?"

"I'd like to keep him. I've always wanted a pet and I understand being shy. I invented the word growing up."

"Doubt it, but go on," he urged when she did that thing to her bottom lip again.

"I really feel like this all happened for a reason. And maybe I'm reaching because I feel sorry for...Pup...but I think he needs me."

"Okay." He had to ask the question. "Why don't you have a pet already?"

"That's easy. I don't have time for one."

"And how will this guy be any different?" He hated how her shoulders deflated even though he wanted to infuse some reality into the situation.

"Right." She exhaled a slow breath.

"And how long will you be in town?"

"Not long. Until I settle my family's affairs and then I'm headed back to Dallas." The next breath she blew out was one of defeat.

Reed muttered a curse. He wanted to make her smile not the other way around. So, continuing this line of questioning wasn't taking him to his happy place. He was looking out for Pup. That much was true. Maybe he could help her think through keeping the dog. She was perfectly capable of making her own decisions. Obviously, she was intelligent. He didn't need to spend a week with her to be able to tell she was sharp. She had impressed him with her quick thinking. She also had a big heart when it came to animals, considering she'd not only been determined to see Pup's medical care through but she was considering giving him a home.

There was a list of admirable qualities in his mind. The fact she'd willingly given up her own life at such a young age to step in to help her mother. Based on what he'd heard so far, she'd been responsible for taking care of the family business, at sixteen years old.

"Okay. Then what? Didn't you take over the deli from your mother?"

"Yes, but maybe I could enlist her help again. She's been more stable now that she's remarried." The hopeful note in her voice told him that had about as much chance of happening as snow in June. Hell, snow in February wasn't a guarantee in this part of Texas, not even a light dusting.

"Believe it or not, I'm not trying to talk you out of it."

"Sounds like it to me," she said under her breath.

"On the positive, you'll be here for a few days maybe weeks. That would give you twenty-four-seven to look after Pup while he heals. He'll need that kind of round-the-clock supervision. I'm guessing the ointment will need to be reapplied and he'll need someone to make sure he doesn't lick it right off before the antibiotic has a chance to do the trick."

"It's a good thing you're not trying to talk me out of this," she retorted with a smile that make him unsure if she was kidding or actually hurt.

"I'm not explaining this right. Let me try this another way. The pup in the other room would be lucky to have you. However, there are some logistics—"

"That don't work," she finished for him. "I'm aware."

"Doesn't mean you can't take him with you."

"Crazy how the heart has a mind of its own, despite logic," she pointed out.

He put his hands up, palms out, in the surrender position. He didn't want to touch that statement with a ten-foot pole.

"I HAVE a lot to do in the next few days. I can't leave the deli forever. My new step-dad isn't cut out for running the show even though he's not the one I left in charge. I shudder to think of the mess I'll be returning to." As much as Addison didn't want to admit it, those words were more than true. Benjamin Davis wasn't competent to run the business her father built. Addison had left her right hand person, Connie Parnassos, in charge.

Her cell buzzed in her purse. She glanced over at Reed. "Sorry. I should check to see who this is."

"Okay." That one word shouldn't send a cold shiver racing down her spine or make her want to explain that it was most likely her mother on the phone.

She reached around in her purse for her phone. She'd hastily thrown it inside when she grabbed her bag earlier. She checked the screen and figured she could put his fears to rest by answering. "Hey, Mom. What's up?"

"Benjamin has a question about where we keep the books and I have no idea what to tell him anymore." Her mother sounded nervous and more than a little on edge. Benjamin could be like a little kid when he didn't get his way. She'd witnessed his actions firsthand.

"Everything okay with you?" she asked her mom.

"Oh, yes. Fine, honey. Benjamin needs to see what the monthly flour bill is. He's being asked to sign for a shipment and thinks we're getting ripped off. He wanted to help and thinks he knows someone who can get dry goods at a better price."

"Tell him to sign for the flour. I'm happy with our supplier." The idea Benjamin wanted to dig his hands into the family business didn't sit well. She'd caught him poking around in the office last week, with the lights out. His kind of 'help' wasn't welcome, and she had to keep her eye on him.

"Well, honey. Listen, he's trying to save money for the business and help you out. You should really use him more. He'd like to be more involved and he is part of the family now."

"I know that. Can we talk about this later? I'm at a vet's office. A dog ran in front of my car and—" She didn't want to point out the fact his marriage to her mother didn't give him the right to go interfering at the deli.

"I hope you didn't admit fault. Benjamin says if you get

into an accident that you shouldn't say you're sorry. People can take that the wrong way and you can end up losing everything." Wasn't Benjamin suddenly lawyer and businessman extraordinaire?

Was it financial security her mother was concerned about? She'd been acting different lately and Addison wondered if the shine wasn't wearing off the new marriage.

"It's nothing like that. He's a stray. He doesn't have an owner as far as we can tell," she said.

"Oh, that's different." Her mother blew out a breath like she was sighing relief.

"Tell Benjamin to sign the invoice. Okay, Mom? We can talk about suppliers when I get back. Nothing needs to change this red-hot minute while I'm away. Plus, I left Connie in charge, so he needs to listen to her."

"Well, if you're sure about the supplier, I'll tell him you're thinking about it for now." Unbelievable that her mother was defending someone she'd known less than a year over her own daughter. But then, Mom had always been a people pleaser. Too bad Addison had never been on the receiving end.

"I'm one hundred percent on this. I have to go now but I'll call later," she promised. Her mother's calls had come less often since the wedding. Having Benjamin work at the deli, even part-time, had been a good way to keep tabs. Or so she'd thought. Having him try to step in and change things wasn't going to cut it.

"Before you hang up, I have an idea," her mother began, and a sinking feeling hit the pit of Addison's stomach.

"Oh, yeah?"

"What if I came back to work at the deli? Took on more of a managerial role?" she asked.

Um...what?

There was no way Addison was going to allow her mother to get back into the daily operations. Addison had to cover her mother's mistakes too many times in the past. When Dad was first gone, Addison understood and never complained about the financials that didn't match invoices. Her mother's attention to detail flew out the window. And even though she was better now, Addison had a sneaky suspicion Benjamin was behind the new interest in taking on more responsibility. He could bowl right over her, whereas Addison didn't budge when he came up with a hair-brained scheme to make more money.

She didn't want to shoot her mother down, though, on the off chance this was genuine and came from her. Not to mention the setback it could cause in their relationship if Addison truly spoke her mind about what a disaster that could be.

"Let's think about it when I get home. Okay?" It wasn't a commitment and it wasn't a rejection. It would also give Addison time to think of a way to let her mother down easily. The last thing she wanted to do was hurt the woman. Despite their differences, Addison loved her mother. Plus, she was the only family left.

"All right. Sounds good." There was a perkiness to her mother's voice that made the let-down that was coming feel worse.

They exchanged goodbyes and Addison exhaled.

"Sorry. Where were we?" She refocused on Reed, tightening her grip around the cell phone in her hand. Out of the corner of her eyes, she'd seen him texting and figured he'd reached out to Declan while she was on the call to her mother.

"You were telling me how much you want to keep the pup in there." He motioned toward the adjacent exam room.

"Yeah, so, about that. You're right. My hands are full back home with my mom and her new husband, who are now trying to 'help' run the business beyond my leave of absence." She couldn't help but roll her eyes. "Sorry. I shouldn't have said that out loud."

"You're fine. No problem. Believe me when I say how well I understand complicated families." His tone revealed there was a story there. But how?

She shot him a look that he took in stride. How could he? The McGannons stuck together. They were a tightknit bunch who had each other's backs. They were basically the envy of everyone in town as far as she could remember.

He'd been generous with his time so far. As she remembered, McGannons were never idle. "You probably have somewhere to be. I'm sorry I've kept you this long."

"I'm good right here." The finality to his tone said he meant it. His deep baritone caused a sensual shiver to race across her skin.

Ignoring it, she asked, "You're good with business problems, right?"

"We do all right." He cracked a smile and she reminded herself that she was talking to one of the most successful cattle ranchers in Texas. His family was wealthy to the tune of millions.

And since she was going all in, she might as well lay it out for him. "My step-dad wants to be part of a business my dad created with my mom. I took over the reins at sixteen and have been doing well ever since. I haven't been perfect and we had an egg supplier who was stealing from us." She glanced up at him and saw a hint of confusion on his face. "We bake our own bread."

"Is this about bread?"

"No, it's about the fact our business has been running

fine with me at the helm and I resent the fact my mom wants to bring an outsider into something my dad created just to get him out of her hair and give the man something to do." There. She said it. No taking it back now. It was out there. Warts and all.

6

Reed cleared his throat before taking a sip of coke. Her words stung in a way they shouldn't have, considering Addison was talking about her family and not his. He looked up to find her studying him.

"Did I say something wrong?"

"No. All good." This wasn't the time to discuss his family troubles. Besides, despite being briefly acquainted with Addison in their youth, he didn't know her well enough to get into the mess that had become his family life. It was only a matter of time before his uncle and cousins gave up on their relationship too. Just like his father.

Rather than get inside his head, Reed shoved the thoughts aside.

"Really? Because I didn't mean to—"

"Nope. You didn't. Plus, we were talking about the pup." He redirected the conversation back on track.

Addison stared at him for a long moment, head cocked to one side.

"Well, I think I was trying to talk myself out of taking the guy home with me but there's no way I would leave him here. I feel responsible for what happened." She put a hand up to stop him from talking. "I do. It was my car that hit him. I'm the reason he's here and suffering."

The finality in her words meant the subject was closed, so Reed didn't argue. He'd made his case already. She could do with it what she pleased. If there was anything he could say to take away some of her guilt, he would in a heartbeat. But he knew the feeling. He'd carried the weight of his father's actions most of his life. Reed knew guilt. He also recognized someone stubbornly holding onto it.

"You have a few hours to decide. You don't have to make a decision right this red-hot minute about the pup," he reminded.

"True." She seemed to be chewing on the thought. He also noticed he used the same phrase she had while on the phone with her mother.

Reed glanced at the clock on the wall, thinking lunch had come and gone. "When was the last time you ate?"

"A while ago." She checked the time and then shook her head. "A few hours, I guess. Why?"

"The pup needs IV fluids and he's on medication so he needs to rest. We can sit in here and go hungry or step out and grab a bite. If you'd rather stick by his side, I understand that too. In that case, I can run out and bring food back." His offer was met with a serious look of contemplation.

"Think we could swing by my aunt and uncle's place? It's been so long since I've been there. My memories are vague. I would like to see what I'm working with, though, since I'll be staying there once he's released. And we could pick up my car. I hate to leave it on the side of the road."

"Deal. I'll just let Derek know the plan. See what time he thinks we should be back." Reed pushed to standing and stepped into the exam room. Derek was standing in the opposite corner, fingers on a keyboard as his assistant stood next to the pup, saying soothing words.

Reed walked to a spot that would put him in Derek's sideview. He glanced over and waved at Reed to join him.

"How long before the pup is able to get up and around or think about leaving?" he asked.

"You know me. I'd prefer to keep him overnight, out of an abundance of caution. But later tonight should be fine. If all goes well, I'd say around eight to nine p.m."

"That should give Addison enough time to get her place ready for him." Reed figured it would also give her time to rethink her decision to take the animal. Pets were a lot of work and responsibility. She had a lot on her plate already considering she was visiting temporarily to sort through her family's things. She might not want the distraction. At the ranch, dogs fit right in. Reed would offer to take the pup if Addison decided she couldn't handle his care. "You'll call me first thing if anything changes about his condition?"

"Absolutely." It went without saying and yet Reed appreciated the confirmation anyway.

"Thank you." He walked over to the pup and leaned over. Those sweet brown eyes stared up at him. The pup was a little loopy. His tongue fell to one side. But he wasn't in any pain based on the look of him. The thought comforted Reed. He leaned over to the pup's ear. "No matter where you end up, you've just found yourself a home. Hang in there, buddy. We'll get you fixed up and back running around, sniffing fire hydrants before you know it."

After stroking the pup's fur, Reed walked over to the office and stood in the doorway. Head down, Addison studied her phone with a frown.

"Everything okay?"

She gasped.

"Yes. Sorry. You surprised me." She blinked up at him and tried to cover the concern on her face that had been there a few seconds ago.

"No need to apologize. I didn't mean to catch you off guard," he said.

"What did your friend say?"

"That we have quite a few hours before the pup is released. What do you think about grabbing a bite to eat?"

"Think we could get something to go? I'd really like to get to my aunt's place and check out the scene. As I remember, stores don't stay open late around here. I need to get settled and get supplies before he's released." She nodded toward the dog.

"At your service." He did a mock bow.

"You've been so nice already. Maybe you should just take me to my car. I can cover everything from there."

Well, he didn't like the turn this conversation had taken and he had no plans to push himself on someone. Still, it didn't seem right to leave her of her own devices since she didn't know anyone in town. "If you don't mind, I'm kind of invested in the outcome of the guy in the next room. I'd like to see it through until he's settled at your place."

"Oh." Her surprise caught him off guard. "Okay. To be honest, having the company is nice. I've been thinking about facing my aunt and uncle's place ever since I was notified. So many mixed emotions and I have no idea what kind of shape the place will be in. Based on what the lawyer said, they moved out a couple of years ago. I'm not sure if I'll be walking into a place filled with cobwebs." She visibly shuddered at the thought.

"Then, please, by all means, allow me to accompany you." He held out his arm.

"I'd like that a lot, actually." She took it and more of that inconvenient electricity surged through him.

His chest squeezed after the way she looked at him. Those cobalt blue honest eyes seemed to look right through him. He should probably be looking for the exit instead of volunteering to stick by her side. But there was something about her that had cracked his carefully constructed walls. And a piece of him that refused to be ignored wanted to find out what that meant.

ADDISON'S CAR was right where they left it on the side of the road. Her heart thumped in her chest as they neared the scene. She reminded herself the pup was going to be fine. The thought another animal had attacked him didn't sit well. The Lab was a hundred pounds, meaning he wasn't exactly a tiny thing. Whatever put those bite marks on him could attack her just as easily. Considering this area was close to her aunt and uncle's place, she reminded herself not to go outside at night alone just to be safe.

"What do you think might have done that to him?" She eyed her vehicle as Reed pulled up beside it.

"Any number of wildlife could be responsible for an attack like that out here." He glanced over at her and seemed to catch on. "But you'll be one hundred percent safe indoors. And if you have to take the trash out at night, I wouldn't worry about it. Until recently, I wouldn't have even advised you to lock the doors."

"Now?" she asked.

"I'd take the precaution. If your family had an alarm system set up, which I doubt, it would have been inactivated when they moved out."

"Right." She took in a breath and shook her head. "It's strange to think of being inside that house without them there."

"I can imagine."

Could he? The ranch was always filled with people coming and going as she remembered.

"Their place isn't too far from here. I was going to volunteer to pick up food and meet you there, but if you'd rather—"

"I'd feel better if you went with me. We probably should have stopped on our way here. You must be starving," she said.

"Miss Penny puts a lunchbox in my hand every time I leave the property. I probably have enough to get us through until we can take a look and see what all you might need to make the place habitable."

"You'll follow me then?" Must be nice to have someone who cared so much. Addison remembered Miss Penny and she remembered her being a sweet person.

"I will."

"Thank you, Reed. For everything you're doing for me and the pup."

"You bet."

Addison exited the truck and moved to her vehicle. There was something daunting about returning to the spot of the accident. Her heart went out to the pup. She glanced around, thinking whatever had attacked him was still out there. Hungry? Ready to attack? She was such a city girl that the notion that a predator could be out there lurking and searching for its next victim caused a cold shiver to race up her spine.

The thought of sleeping in her aunt's house alone suddenly didn't seem like the great idea it had when all she could think about was getting a break from the Dallas and the deli. The city was great, don't get her wrong, but the recent addition to the family felt like a lot coming at her all at once. There were days Addison wished life would just slow down so she could enjoy it more. Maybe date more. It was probably her mother's wedding that had her suddenly thinking about how alone she felt.

Addison climbed behind the wheel and navigated back onto the road. Her aunt's house wasn't far according to GPS, despite the signal cutting in and out. She remembered all the time she'd lost cell phone connection at her relatives' place. It hadn't bothered her when she was younger. Now, it felt like someone was about to cut off her arm. Funny how dependent she'd become on having a signal.

Hopefully, she would still have one.

Driving up to the two-story home with a wraparound porch, it struck her just how empty the place felt to her now. She wasn't sure what she had expected to find, considering the place had been empty for a couple of years.

There were no ridiculous goats wandering around the property. No chickens. The place had once been alive with animals and people. Her aunt would be standing on the porch, waving, the minute she heard the truck pull onto the blacktop road. Addison blinked through blurry eyes. She sniffed away tears as reality struck like a physical blow. Her beloved aunt and uncle were gone.

Her next thought was about Ivy. Her cousin would want to know her parents had passed away. Maybe there were clues about her whereabouts in her room or somewhere in the house. Surely, someone knew where she was or what had happened to her. There had to be a trail somewhere. With laptops, social media, and cell phones, people didn't just fall off the face of the earth anymore.

Addison pulled up next to the once-vibrant home. She'd thought to have the electricity turned on before she made the trip down. Good thinking on her part. She couldn't imagine staying in a dark house for the next week or two. The thought of bringing the pup here for company alone sounded better and better the more she thought about it.

Reed pulled in behind her. He exited his truck and then stood at the driver's side door, digging out a small cooler from his backseat. He held it up before closing the door and meeting her at the side entrance to the porch.

The clock on her dashboard said it was already three o'clock in the afternoon. Her stomach growled as she stepped onto the first stair of the wooden porch. It creaked and she hoped it covered the embarrassing noise from her stomach.

"It's strange to be back here without them. I half expect my aunt to bound out the front door and pull me into one of those warm hugs. I swear she always smelled like cookies."

"She was one of the kindest people I've personally ever met." Reed's kind words meant so much.

Taking a deep breath, she fisted the key to the front door that had been sent by the lawyer. "Here goes nothing."

After unlocking the door, she opened it. Her heart took another hit when she stepped inside. All the furniture was covered with sheets, like the occupants would be returning after a long winter.

A sob bubbled up and out of Addison's throat. She mumbled an apology as Reed took her by the arm. She turned to him. He set the cooler down next to his boots and then hauled her against his chest, where she let a few tears fall.

"Don't ever be sorry for caring about people so much that it hurts when they're gone." He stroked her hair as he spoke and it was the most touching, intimate moment of her life. She realized how little she'd been living based on the sheer electricity zinging between them, even now. Even in the midst of the tenderness he was showing.

"My emotions are catching me off guard." She figured this reminded her a little bit about when her father died—an event she still wasn't sure her young brain had been capable of processing. She'd cried. And then shoved her emotions aside without even realizing that was what she was doing. It was survival at its most basic. Her young brain couldn't comprehend what was happening, so she'd forged ahead.

"It's okay. You've only just heard."

"I hate that I didn't see them one more time. You know?" She wiped away the last rogue tears rolling down her cheeks.

"Understandable. Your life was busy in Dallas."

"True. I love working in the business my father created. It makes me feel connected to him even though he's been gone for years at this point. But lately, I've been feeling like I'm missing out on something else out there. I'm always nose to the grindstone and I can't help but think maybe if I wasn't, I would have known about my aunt and uncle. I would have paid more attention to what was going on with my cousin. I'm thinking that maybe I'm focused on the wrong things. Does that make any sense?"

She searched his eyes for understanding and found more than that, she saw a reflection. A kindred spirit. And her heart squeezed because after a couple of weeks at the most, she had a business to get back to.

7

Reed couldn't give answers to questions he hadn't figured out for himself. He pulled a sheet off the sofa, shook the dust out on the front porch, and then placed it over the rug in the living room.

The place looked like he'd stepped into a time warp. The home and its furnishings had been well preserved. There was a reclining sofa and a pair of rocking chairs with a coffee table anchoring them. There were hurricane lamps on matching side tables. The TV had a back. He wondered if he could even pull up a game on it. Of course, there'd be no satellite service hooked up.

He flipped on a light. It worked. Then, he set about opening curtains and pulling up blinds to shower the room in sunlight while Addison set up a makeshift picnic on the floor.

"I had the electricity turned back on since I'll be staying here for a while," she said.

"How long?"

She shrugged a shoulder. "Until I'm done." She issued a sharp sigh. "It's strange to think about closing out someone's life. You know? I mean, we spend all this time building a life with someone and then all the stuff is left for others to pick through and decide what's important and what can be trashed."

"My mom died when I was so young that I honestly don't remember much about her. There are bits and pieces here and there. I wonder how much I actually remember about her versus what I've been told. But I have this necklace of hers. It was special to her, or so I'm told. I keep it next to my bed locked safely in a box. Every once in a while," he sat down, "I take it out and imagine her wearing it. How much the emeralds must have sparkled. How happy she must have been when she wore it out. It makes me feel a little bit closer to her. Or, at least, it did."

"Not now?" Her eyebrow arched and she stopped opening containers.

"I can't remember the last time I took it out. It's been a couple of years at least. And yet, knowing it's there makes me feel like a piece of her is still around, still with me."

"I always looked at your family like you guys had it so easy." There was so much compassion in her eyes. "There are so many of you and you're all so close."

He nodded.

"It never occurred to me that your mother was gone and you have the same pain as everyone else."

"Most people only ever saw us from the outside looking in. I'd be lying if I said I wasn't grateful to grow up in a loving home with lots of family around. Missing my mother and not knowing my father very well is the same pain other people experience, but my uncle did the best he could to make me and my brothers feel like we belonged. Until recently, I did too."

"What happened recently?" She blinked at him, confusion darkening those eyes.

She was the first person he actually could see himself talking to about it, but he'd said enough about his family already.

"Talk about it later, okay?"

"Yeah. Sure." Did a wall just come up between them? Damn.

"I do want to tell you. But right now, we'll run out of daylight if we're not careful and stores will close, and I'd like to help get you set up for the pup, if that's all right with you."

"All right? Are you kidding me? I'd pay good money for help." She smiled and some of the tension eased. "Plus, this sandwich is amazing."

"That's Miss Penny."

"I vaguely remember thinking she might be the best cook I've ever been around and my aunt was no slouch. I incorporated her version of potato salad at the deli and it was a huge hit. People still come in for that dish alone in summer." She had a wistful quality now.

"I may have eaten that once at a potluck. I'd have to agree. Your aunt's cooking rivaled Miss Penny's."

"Oh, and the baking she did. Cookies from scratch." She made an mmmm sound. "The pies she made were insane."

"I do remember those from holiday potlucks." Reed smiled. He figured he could walk the house after dinner and see if there was anything she needed. He was already making a mental checklist for pup supplies. Fortunately, Derek would have food and basics, like a collar and leash.

They chatted easily while finishing up sandwiches and the soup Miss Penny had packed for him. She'd thought to pack a bottle of water and a coke, which he offered to Addison.

"Only if you share." She hopped up and disappeared into the kitchen. "Reed." There was fear in her voice that got him up and moving in two shakes.

"What is it?" He was in the kitchen before she could answer. He followed her gaze to the back door. A pane had been broken and the back door was ajar.

He crossed the room and instinctively positioned himself between her and the door. "Could be kids. Teenagers are always looking for a place to make out or party."

"Yes. That's true." She was frozen to the spot and her breath had quickened.

"I can patch it up. I'm sure your uncle has supplies either in here or the barn."

"The barn. He always kept his tools there."

"Do you still want to stay here?" The question had to be asked.

"This is the only place I have. I planned on staying here. I mean, yes, I do want to be here. I'll be able to work longer if I'm here and wake up...I'm rambling. It's what I do when I'm freaking out inside."

"There's no reason to panic. I'm here. I can stay the night if you'd like. Help you get settled with the house and the pup."

"You would do that?" She blinked big eyes at him.

"It would give me a break from dealing with everything we have going on at home." It was gospel truth. He also didn't want her to feel indebted to him for an act of kindness. They should be the norm but weren't always.

She stared at him for a long moment before turning to face him, pushing up on her tiptoes, and touching her lips to his. A bolt of lightning struck and his skin scorched where it made contact with hers. He flexed his fingers a couple of times trying to ease some of the tension stringing his muscles taut. He had to fight every instinct inside him to kiss her back because he knew, without a doubt, it would be a slippery slope. Willpower wasn't normally an issue for Reed, so the fact he had to pull on every ounce of strength he had not to claim those pink lips of hers caught him off guard.

"I hope that wasn't out of line." She blinked up at him and her eyes were glittery with something that looked a lot like need. The attraction simmering between them surged and he had to suppress the urge to claim those full cherry lips of hers.

"You're fine," was all he said. All he could say. His life was complicated. She was only here for a week or two, give or take. There couldn't be much more than a casual friendship between them despite the chemistry trying to convince him otherwise. Despite the ache that had suddenly formed in his chest. And despite how much he wanted to feel her silky skin against his.

Besides, he wasn't in the right mental space to start up anything with anyone, especially not someone who could make his pulse race faster than an Indy driver on a hot track just by standing next to him. Reed didn't do more than casual flings with like-minded women. He didn't do serious or lose his mind to attraction. And he didn't normally have conversations in his head like this either, but here he was.

ADDISON TOOK A STEP BACK. Her emotions were running on full tilt, causing her to do something she would never consider doing under normal circumstances—randomly kiss a guy. She'd gone with her instinct instead of allowing her brain to talk her out of it like she normally would. Not that she went around wanting to kiss guys she barely knew all the time. Whatever. She was flustered because the second her lips touched his, she realized her mistake. One kiss would most certainly not be enough with Reed McGannon.

Thankfully, he hadn't urged more. It wouldn't have taken much coaxing, and kissing Reed wasn't something she could afford to focus on right now. Sure would be an amazing distraction, though. She smiled just a little at the thought. It was so true. Addison had become so good at keeping her head down and focusing on work, that she'd neglected having much of a personal life. She rarely ever went for what she wanted, and she'd wanted to press her lips to Reed's.

Reed cleared his throat. They both stood there for a long moment, comfortable instead of awkward despite the air being charged with electricity around them.

"I'll check the rest of the house." Reed's voice was low, gravelly, and made her stomach drop like she'd jumped from a plane skydiving.

There was great satisfaction in knowing she'd affected him in a similar fashion. Because the kiss, brief as it had been, was the new barometer for first kisses in her book. And a little thrill of excitement tickled her that she'd actually gone for it.

"Should I stay here?" she asked.

"Might be best. Make sure no one comes through the backdoor." He walked over, closed the door and locked it. "I know it isn't much, but it would take an intruder a few extra seconds to get in and me time to get to you."

"Okay." The thought of someone coming through the

back door while they were in the house sent a shiver racing down her back.

"If my guess is right about the teenagers, they would be detoured by the vehicles parked outside."

Reading between the lines, he seemed to be saying it wouldn't come to a confrontation. She walked to the drawer and pulled out her aunt's biggest butcher knife anyway.

Reed smiled before disappearing down the hallway, leaving Addison to reacquaint herself with the house. It had been built before open concept was a thing, so the eat-in kitchen was in the back of the home. Stairs leading upstairs were at the front of the house. There was a landing with a half bath to the right. No bedrooms downstairs, two up. It had been the perfect size for the family of three. Being inside the house again brought an onslaught of memories.

Addison figured she needed to make herself comfortable if she was to stay here. She pulled the sheet off the dining table and chairs that seated four. A dust cloud filled the room. She waved her free hand around to cut into the fog before making her way to the back door. She shook the sheet out on the edge of the porch in back. Another dust cloud billowed before being carried off in the breeze.

She looked out onto the backyard. The chicken coop was in need of repair and the barn looked to be standing on its last leg. Weathered from neglect. After the dust had settled, she took in a breath, thinking how much she remembered being able to breathe in Cattle Cove. Was it the unconditional love she felt from her aunt and uncle that had been sorely missing at home? Was it all the happy childhood memories that made this place feel so special? Or was it because her father had been alive and she hadn't had a care in the world? Her life had been lonely in Dallas with her parents gone until after dinner seven days a week. That was the nature of owning a business, she realized once she stepped in to take over for her dad. But when she was here at the farm, as they'd called it, she was surrounded by people and animals. Everything felt more alive here. There was so much happiness and great memories. And so she was even more confused by the fact her cousin willingly walked away from it all.

By the time Addison stepped inside the kitchen, Reed's footsteps could be heard in the hallway. The wood flooring groaned underneath his feet. A few of those boards would need to be fixed before the sale. She looked around the room, thinking all good things must come to an end.

"I didn't find any damage to windows or rooms upstairs. In fact, all the coverings were still on the beds and furniture." His report surprised her.

"When we came in through the living room there was no sign anyone had been inside the home. Isn't that strange?"

"It rules out rowdy teenagers," he said.

"Someone came in quietly and didn't want their presence to be obvious." Her mind snapped to one name. "Could it have been Ivy?"

"It's possible. Nothing seems out of place. The house wasn't ransacked. Whoever came in might have been looking for something specific," he said.

"She may not have known where to find what she was looking for but she would have an idea." Addison thought about the little desk her aunt had made for the laundry room off the kitchen. The laundry room door was to her left. She crossed the room, making a beeline toward it. The room was long, skinny, and off to the side of the house. At the time this house was built, it would have been the kitchen and those were often away from the main living spaces due to the heat from early stoves and general lack of air conditioning. Fire was a real threat with cooking in the days this house was built.

Reed was on her heels as she opened the door.

"Come to think of it, I don't think I've ever seen this door shut before." In fact, her aunt was often inside writing letters or paying bills as she used to say. She was the financial brains of the family, she'd joke.

She'd move in and out from the kitchen to her private space, dancing in between. Looking around now, her aunt and uncle didn't have much but they always seemed happy.

"Is it odd this place seems so much smaller than I remembered it?" Her perspective had changed.

"That's the funny thing about visiting a place as a kid and then coming back later. I remember my uncle used to take us skiing once a year. It was just a small hill in New Mexico. Not to me when I was little, though. It was the biggest mountain I'd ever set my eyes on."

His smile was devastating and she had to remind herself to breathe. "My brothers and I went back a couple of years ago and couldn't believe we ever considered it a mountain."

"It's crazy how perspective changes as we grow up." She also realized that was true for expectations. Sometimes life dealt blows that made it hard to trust anyone again.

The desk, tucked in the corner past the washer and dryer, was the only piece of furniture in the house that wasn't covered by a sheet.

"Did you notice—"

"I sure did." His confirmation sent another icy chill racing down her spine.

"Okay." The drawers were all closed but there was considerably less dust on the desk. "Whoever did this came here recently."

"That's my guess," he said.

"I wonder if my aunt and uncle had the locks changed once Ivy ran away."

"Skinner would have been sheriff at the time. I doubt he would have kept a record of a runaway, but I'll ask Sheriff Justice if she knows anything." He pulled out his cell and fired off a text.

Must be nice to have the sheriff's number so easily accessible. Then again, maybe not. He did say a lot had been going on at the ranch and that might signal trouble if he was in close contact with the sheriff. She made a mental note to circle around to that conversation again later.

Addison bent down and scanned the desk. The handmade job was actually nice.

"I don't see anything out of the ordinary. Think I should open a drawer?" It also occurred to her that a break-in had occurred. They would have to call the sheriff and Addison didn't want to cover up any fingerprints.

Reed looked around for something she could use and then shook his head. He squatted down so he could check the mechanics underneath the drawers. "That's simple." He reached a hand deep underneath the middle drawer and as his hand came back, the drawer came with it.

"It's messy. That's not like my aunt. She organized her spices alphabetically."

"Whoa. As organized as Miss Penny is, I don't think she'd ever go that far."

"I don't know what I'm looking for but I can tell you that I believe someone has been in this drawer, moving papers around."

"Would Ivy come home after her parent's death to check for a will or something valuable?" he asked.

"I'm surprised she didn't know her parents had an attorney." But then Ivy disappearing at all was a shock. So, should she really be caught off guard by anything that has happened since?

"They might not have thought they would need one years ago when she was around."

She nodded. Fair point.

"They may have believed she was capable of being executor at some point later on down the road. And then she ended up getting mixed up with something or someone. There could have been strife in the family."

"It's just hard to fathom. To me, they lived an idyllic life."

Reed looked at her with the most serious eyes and said, "What families look like on the outside aren't always reflective of what's happening on the inside."

Of course, he was right. And, based on his expression, the personal story behind those words carried a lot of pain.

8

"Is it against the law to break into your own home?"

"Technically, this is your home now." Reed had no idea what the legal ramifications were.

"The break-in seems to be recent but there are a couple of problems. For one, I've only technically owned this house for a few days and I haven't even figured out the probate process yet. So, I have no idea where I stand legally. Plus, the break-in might have happened before it belonged to me and, therefore, the complainants would have to file a complaint. Right?" She threw her hands up. "Plus, I'm not even sure if anything's missing. Whoever did this might not have found what they wanted. I don't know what my aunt's possessions were other than a gold wedding band that she was buried with. They were simple people, so I can't imagine they were stockpiling gold bars here at the house."

"A lot of people hide cash in their houses in these parts. Some don't completely trust banks, not with all their money. You'd be surprised at how many people stick money under their mattresses."

Addison laughed despite the tension in her taut face

muscles. Or maybe it was because of the tension she needed a mental break.

"It's not funny. Nothing is funny right now. Except that I had this cartoon-like image of old people stuffing money under their mattresses and it cracked me up."

"You're probably not too far off the mark." He laughed too. "And with a shotgun next to the bedpost. Although, to be fair, the shotgun is probably recent."

Addison took in a slow breath.

"Since we don't know what we're looking for and I'm not even sure if a crime was committed here, should we move on?"

"Yes. I sent the sheriff a text and…" His cell buzzed. He checked the screen. "She'll stop by in half an hour. Until then, I'll board up the window. Did you touch the doorknob?"

"I'm afraid so. Both sides."

"Okay, then it's safe to say I won't be messing with evidence. And we have the desk here as well. If this was an amateur smash and grab deal, then there might be prints to go off of."

"What if it was her? Ivy, I mean." Addison's eyes were saucers. "It's strange to think she'd grown estranged with her family to the point of sneaking around and breaking in her childhood home."

"It might be the person she's with if…" He stopped himself before finishing the sentence but the unspoken words hung in the air anyway. *She's still alive.*

"It's probably just a hope, of course. But I would love for her to come walking through that door right now."

"You know, the person you described isn't the same person I remember. I thought she mostly kept to herself. Had her nose in a book." He followed her out of the long room and into the kitchen again. He pulled out his phone and checked the screen. "Declan is basically saying the same thing. The two hung out a little bit over two summers. She was nice. That was about it."

She nodded. "It's a shame someone didn't know her better."

"You said tools were in the barn. Can you point me in a direction?" he asked.

"That way." She put her hands on his arms. His back was to her. And then she walked him toward the back door, which he carefully opened in case a print could still be lifted.

Addison stood at the back door as he crossed the yard to the barn. It was in need of repair. As were quite a few things around the house, he'd noticed as he walked through the rooms, checking windows and locks.

He could feel her eyes on him now, and he'd had to ignore the electrical impulses still vibrating through his arms, aftershocks from her touch. The barn door had a lock on it but the boards were loose and he easily shoved one out of the way and gained access. Light peeked through the cracks but it wasn't enough to see clearly and he figured there were all kinds of spiders and snakes inside. Probably field mice as well. He palmed his cell and turned on the flashlight app.

The barn looked like something out of a haunted house. Spiderwebs practically everywhere. A scurrying noise to his left. He shined the light in the general direction of where it came from, but probably didn't want to know what was responsible for the sound in all fairness. He waved his hand, left to right, like a wand.

Thankfully, the red Coleman was tucked beside the door. Easy in. Easy out. He crawled on all fours, and then shoved the toolbox out first. Years of neglect had decayed the barn and the chicken coop had been in a similar state when he passed by it. For Addison to sell this place, it was going to need a lot of spit shine.

He crawled out of the barn, figuring he had at least one cobweb in his hair. He gave a little shiver because spiders had always given him the heebie-jeebies. He was as tough as they came in any situation until he walked into a spiderweb.

Reed palmed the handle and hurried to the house. Time was getting away from them and there was a lot to do before they swung by Derek's office to pick up the pup.

The sound of tires on pavement shifted his path. He held a hand up for Addison to stay put. A lot of good that did. She had a look of determination that made him admire her even more as she joined him. Under the circumstances, he shouldn't crack a grin. And yet, that's exactly what happened.

He set the toolbox down and linked their fingers, an instinctive move he questioned almost immediately after as if crossing a line. He wouldn't have been surprised if she'd pulled back and was surprisingly comforted when she didn't. The chemistry pinging between them reminded him of the kiss. There'd never been something so powerful in something so seemingly innocent. A quick peck was all it had amounted to despite feeling the ground shift underneath his feet.

The sheriff parked and then stepped out of her vehicle.

"Afternoon, Sheriff Justice," Reed said. "This is my friend, Addison Lowery. She is the niece of Mr. and Mrs. Murray and has inherited their place."

"Pleasure to meet you, Ms. Lowery." Sheriff Justice extended her hand. The two shook and then so did her and Reed.

"Please, call me Addison. When I hear Ms. Lowery, I look over my shoulder to see if my mother is standing there." Warmth came through in Addison's voice.

"Will do, Addison. Only if you'll call me Laney."

"Deal."

"Can you tell me what happened and show me the area of the break-in?"

"Right this way." Addison reached out for Reed's hand this time, and he linked their fingers as they walked to the back door.

They gave the sheriff the run-through and she studied the knob. She followed them into the laundry room and examined the desk without touching it.

"I think I'm up to date on what's going on here. No matter who owns the premises, it's still a break-in. Nothing was damaged other than the broken window and we don't know if anything was stolen, so I'll file a damage report," Laney reported.

"At least we'll get something on record."

"I'll dust for prints and see if anything comes up there. We don't have a lot of vagrants in Cattle Cove, but there's a possibility someone was traveling through and wanted shelter for a night or two. The person might have come across what they viewed as an abandoned house and decided to stay overnight." Fair points.

"What about Ivy Murray?"

"I know the family. They had a good reputation in town. I didn't know her personally, but if there's a file on her disappearance, I'll see what I can learn from it and get back to you." The sheriff's cell buzzed. "Excuse me for one second."

She walked out of earshot to take the call.

"Maybe we'll get a print and know if Ivy came back." Call it wishful thinking, but Addison couldn't help but think it would kill two birds with one stone. Okay, bad word choice. She didn't want to 'kill' anything or throw any rocks. But she'd take anything that could lead her to Ivy's whereabouts or prove that she was still alive.

"What about a computer?" Reed asked. "Did your aunt have a laptop or cell phone?"

"Everything is still at the rest home. I didn't have the will to pick it up on my way here, so I told them to find a way to wipe out the hard drive and clean off the phone to donate them both." She could add that she didn't think she would need any of it. "Let me give them a call to see if they've done it already."

Reed nodded.

Addison moved into the living room and sat on the floor at their picnic spot. The house had a musty, unused smell. Even with the blinds and curtains opened, the place felt lifeless and empty.

Having the pup here would bring new life. There was still a laundry list of things to do to get ready and the break-in was absorbing the day. She pulled out her cell phone and realized she had a couple of texts from her mother.

*Are you sure about the supplier?*

*Maybe you should give Benjamin a chance.*

*Addy?*

Addison never like being called Addy. She didn't have the heart to tell her mother or the patience because the name seemed to surface when her mother needed something from her. She took in a breath and rolled her shoulders, trying to ease some of the strain. Thinking about the man her mother married caused tension knots to form in her neck and shoulders.

She pulled up the number to the rest home.

"Graceful Acres, Billie speaking. How may I help you?" The voice was as southern as they came, but Addison's interactions with Billie had been pleasant. She had a way of emoting sympathy through her lilt that was comforting.

"Billie, hi. It's Addison again."

"Oh, hi." Billie gave the impression the two were lifelong friends.

"I have a question that might sound odd."

"Shoot."

"Are any of my aunt and uncle's tech still there? I can't remember their directions and I don't have the paperwork in front of me."

"Um, let me check on that, hon." Billie called everyone hon and yet she pulled it off without sounding offensive or condescending.

"Okay." Addison waited while she was on hold. She started making a mental list of all the dog supplies she would need. Leash. Collar. Food. Water. Bowls. Although, she could use one of her aunt's baking dishes in a pinch. What else? Gauze. That should do it. Right? Then there was the supply list she needed. She would need to check the cabinets to see what she was working with in the form of dishes and pans, but she needed some form of caffeine and a way to brew it. Her current addiction was cold brew and she wondered if she could get that out here. Her suitcase was still in the car but that was mostly toiletries and enough clothes to last a few days since there was a washer and dryer. She'd packed four pairs of shoes that suddenly seemed like overkill. Packing in a rush while dealing with the blow of losing her beloved aunt and uncle didn't result in the best luggage choices. It was still shocking to learn how quickly her aunt's condition had deteriorated and Uncle Bridie, who died grief-stricken. The last part didn't surprise her considering how much in love the two had been.

"Hon?"

"Yes. Still here."

"Thanks for holding so long. Those devices have not been cleaned yet. Do you want us to pack them up in the boxes with Mr. and Mrs. Murray's other belongings?"

Relief washed over her and a glimmer of hope took seed.

"Yes. Please. I'll be by as soon as I can get a truck to pick those up."

"Take your time. They'll be here whenever you're ready."

"Thank you. I'll most likely come by tomorrow." She needed to rent a truck, which she didn't figure would be too difficult here. She'd already been warned her aunt had taken a few pieces of furniture to the home to make it feel more like hers.

"Sounds like a plan."

"Thanks again, Billie. I appreciate everything you're doing and did for my aunt and uncle."

"Not a problem, hon. Truth be told, they were one of my favorite couples. It warms the heart to know they went together, if you know what I mean." Billie sniffed before clearing her throat. "If I could find a man that loved me like that, I wouldn't be twice divorced."

"They had quite a bond." Addison said goodbye and ended the call. She sniffed back her own tears. She'd become a leaky faucet lately. She straightened her shoulders and returned to the kitchen where Reed was sitting in a chair, staring at his cell. "They're intact. Maybe we'll find something in her e-mail or on her phone."

The sheriff was busy with a kit, lifting prints from the doorknob.

"When do you want to pick them up?" he asked.

"It's getting late and we still need to pick up Pup, so I figured tomorrow might be the best time. I need to rent a truck anyway since there's more than my car can handle. Figured I'd do it in one fell swoop." The last thing she wanted was a lot of back and forth with the home. It was hard to imagine her relatives there, separated from the place they loved so much. Away from their animals. Away from everything familiar they'd built from scratch.

Addison's cell buzzed in her hand. She checked the screen. More texts from her mother. More with the pleas to let Benjamin do things his way. More desperate sounding each time.

Seriously?

Why was her mother beginning to sound so desperate over a flour supplier? And why was she suddenly so interested in the family business?

9

"I'll let you know if there's a file on Ivy and whether or not I was able to lift a print." Sheriff Justice stood at the kitchen door, her kit tucked under her arm, cell phone in hand.

Reed thanked her and then tucked his own cell away. The supplies he'd requested would arrive in a few minutes.

"Ever have so much to do, you don't even know where to start?" Addison took a deep breath.

"Every day." He cracked a smile and was rewarded with one in return. The shot to his heart was well worth it. And then he said, "And I'm guessing so do you. You run a successful business."

"Well, speaking of which, Benjamin is trying to change things while I'm gone. I've barely been away a day and he's trying to get his fingers in the business my father started." She paced in the kitchen. "I have to be away and it's not great to think everything I've built for my father's memory might be shredded in a few days if I don't hurry back." She started snapping her fingers. "Maybe I should go back home and come here on weekends. Spread this out over time instead of trying to go through all this in a week or two."

Her stress levels were rising, based on the flush to her cheeks. The rosy hue only served to make her more beautiful. He didn't speak, figuring she didn't need someone to step in and try to fix her problems, especially someone who didn't know anything about running her deli or her family situation. So, he listened.

"But then it'll be harder to find Ivy," she reasoned. "And then there's the pup. He needs to be here in case a family tries to claim him."

Over Reed's dead body. He kept that part to himself.

"I can't pretend to know what you're going through or how to solve your problems," He began. "I know ranching and my family is about as complicated as they come lately."

She stopped and leaned a hip against the counter.

"You're determined and strong. I personally wouldn't want to butt heads with you. You have a vision for your family's business, for continuing your father's legacy, and I doubt anyone will be able to shake it."

She cocked her head to one side, listening. She exhaled and rolled her shoulders.

"You'll figure this out and get a handle on it. As far as your aunt and uncle's home, there are folks who can handle that too if you'd rather stay in Dallas. My guess is that you want to be here. You want to be the one going through their belongings, because you care about family more than you care about yourself."

"I feel like I'm letting everyone down. Like I have a loose grip on things as it is and one slip means it'll all be over," she admitted.

"I may not know much about your situation, but there's

no way you'd allow that to happen. There's too much fight in you."

"It means more than you know to hear you say that." She should hear this every day. He couldn't imagine her not having people in her life who told her those words all the time. She deserved to hear them.

The sound of a vehicle coming down the drive caused her to tense.

"What's that?" she asked, a look of concern on her face.

Reed stood up and checked out the window. "The cavalry."

"I have no idea what that means, but I like the sound of it." She followed him to the window.

"I hope you don't mind. I figured you could use a hand getting some basic supplies in here, plus getting ready for the pup, who will be on his way shortly."

"Are you kidding?" The shock in her voice hit him in a deep place. "No one has ever done anything like this for me before. I don't know what to say or how to thank you even."

"You can thank me by accepting the help and paying it forward when you can."

"Deal. I can't help but think I'm getting off easy here." She practically beamed and he loved being the one to put a smile on her face after everything she'd been through.

"You have enough on your mind trying to deal with the loss of your loved ones. This is nothing."

For the second time, she pushed up to her tiptoes and pressed a kiss to his lips. This time, he kissed her back, long and slow. She tasted like honey and all he could think was how easy it would be for him to get used to this. But he decided not to read too much into it, so he pulled back. Heightened emotions weren't the best platform by which to hop into a relationship. And besides, no matter how attracted he might be to Addison, she was a short-timer here. No sooner than they get past their first real kiss, because what had happened so far was nothing more than a tease, and she'd be headed back to Dallas where she needed to be in order to preserve her father's legacy.

Reed understood about legacies, the good and the bad.

So, trying to date with that many miles between them and responsibilities would be an exercise in frustration. He didn't do long distance. Better to nip this thing in the bud.

"Thank you, Reed." She threw her hands up in the air but the spark in her eyes was all he needed.

"Let's go open the front door and let them get started setting up."

"Okay."

She followed him through the house before opening the door where she stopped. He sidestepped her and welcomed Ranch Foreman Hawk, Miss Penny, and Levi.

"Thank you for coming," he said to the trio. This morning's event was the last thing on his mind, despite knowing he would have to face his father sooner or later. This seemed like a good reason to push off the meeting. He hadn't exactly made any promises.

"Wouldn't miss it." Miss Penny's arms were filled with stackable containers of food. The genuine smile on her face meant there were going to be some amazing meals in Addison's near future. "I packed up some of those butter cookies you love."

Reed didn't want to get into the fact that she seemed to realize he was spending the night. And he especially didn't want to acknowledge Miss Penny's ear-to-ear grin. Since pointing out he was only there as a friend might stick him in the category of *Thou dost protest too much*, he decided to force a smile back. "What can I help with?"

"There are a few more containers in mine and Hawk's..." She caught herself, and an awkward look followed by a serious blush pushed him over to the *they have to be dating* side. Levi shot him a look that said he was in the same camp. Reed couldn't help but notice it was the first time since the whole ordeal with their fathers started the two of them were on the same side of anything.

No. That wasn't entirely fair. They'd all agreed on welcoming Kurt into the family too. Of course, as the weeks droned on with Uncle Clive in a coma, tensions had thickened.

"I'll just..." Reed stopped right there as an embarrassed Miss Penny blew out a breath and then walked toward the porch.

Hawk followed with fresh pillows, sheets, and blankets in his hands.

"We packed fresh towels and a bag for you in case you decided to sleep over." Levi pressed his lips together like he was clamping his mouth shut before he said the rest.

"We're friends," Reed said before he could stop himself.

"Yeah. I know." Levi walked by and Reed was certain he heard a small laugh. Just because all of Reed's cousins had found relationships and were settling down didn't mean the bug was going to hit this side of the family.

So many words came to mind, but Reed figured leaving the topic alone was the best course of action. As he walked up to the passenger side of the opened door of the truck, he realized what Levi thought was so funny.

Red lipstick.

Yep. There it was plain as the nose on Reed's face. It was way too late to backtrack but he immediately wiped the red stain from his lips. It did, however, remind him of her citrus and floral scent that reminded him of fresh flowers after a spring rain.

Now that he was waxing poetic, he figured he'd trade in his Stetson for a fedora. He grabbed the extra containers and his forearms froze as he carried the meals inside. He tucked them in the freezer, certain the fact he could look Levi in the eyes after wiping off the lipstick was a dead giveaway.

The trio left the house for another round and since Reed figured the cat was out of the bag anyway, he walked over to Addison and brought her into a bone-melting kiss. He thrust his tongue inside her mouth as his pulse jacked through the roof. He pulled back long enough to see hers pounding at the base of her throat. So, he dipped his head and pressed a kiss there too before the others joined them.

"You have..." She blinked up at him with those gorgeous eyes of hers.

"I know. Lipstick." He tore a paper towel off the rack and wiped it off. "They saw it earlier, so."

It was Addison's turn to blush. And she was all the prettier for it.

WITHIN THE TIMEFRAME of two hours, all the sheets had been removed from furniture pieces and were somewhere in the wash cycle, tables had been dusted, and floors had been mopped. The house came alive with the five of them, each sweeping through room by room until the place was clean and bright again, musty smell replaced with that of fresh-cut flowers.

The crew worked with the efficiency of a well-oiled engine, polishing and adjusting, fixing the door after loading the fridge and freezer. A proper dog bed was set up for the pup and the sofa had been converted into a makeshift bed.

For the first time in a very long time, Addison felt a lightness in her chest that bordered on joy. She had a team at the deli and the place ran well most of the time. There was such a huge difference in the feeling of people showing up in the spirit of neighborly help versus people who punched a timecard and worked by the hour, watching the clock and counting down the minutes until they were free.

As the clock closed in on eight o'clock, Levi, Hawk, and Miss Penny gathered up their empty bags.

"It's time we took off," Levi said before everyone took turns with hugs.

Reed held onto Levi a few seconds longer than the others. "I appreciate this, Levi."

"Any time. I mean it." Levi looked to Addison after the pair broke apart. "We're here for both of you any time you need us. I mean that. Don't be afraid to take me up on the offer."

"Will do." Addison was a little overwhelmed by the sincere gesture. "And thank you for everything you've done."

"Your aunt and uncle were kind people. I'm sorry for your loss."

The air felt sucked out of the room and Addison had to remind herself to breathe. "Thank you, Levi."

She remembered him as being one of the nicest people she'd met while in town. All the McGannons had those drop-dead gorgeous looks, underwear model bodies, and sense of honor. Call it cowboy code but she couldn't imagine any one of them looking the other way if someone needed a hand.

"My pleasure." He locked gazes with Reed. "Are we okay?"

Reed's response didn't come immediately. He studied his cousin for a long moment. His gaze never wavering. When he spoke, there was a vulnerability to his voice that he hadn't shown before and it melted her heart a little bit.

"I think so."

"That's good enough for me. For now," Levi said.

After another round of hugs, Miss Penny and Hawk excused themselves. Levi quickly followed. Before she could ask Reed what he and Levi were talking about, another vehicle came up the drive. She recognized it immediately as Derek's.

Before she could process all the kind acts, Reed was on the front porch and she was a half-step behind.

Within another fifteen minutes, the dog was settled onto his bed in the living room. The mattress sat on the floor with one of those child-safety fences to keep the pup from moving around too much.

They met Derek who transported the Lab into his new spot. The minute he was settled, Addison was struck by just how much this place felt like home again. She chalked it up to having an animal around combined with the efforts of Reed's family. Her aunt had always kept a clean house despite a menagerie of pets that were technically supposed to live outside but seemed to be indoors more than not.

The Lab looked up at her as she moved the pen. Those sweet, weary eyes. Careful to make her movements deliberate, she sat down near him. A couple of feet should give him the space he needed. Ears back with his tail tucked between his legs, he showed signs of fear. A scared dog in a new environment meant she needed to tread lightly.

Ivy spent more time around animals than Addison. Her

cousin would know what to do. She would have the experience that Addison so sorely lacked to make this guy feel at home.

Reed walked Derek out and she'd zoned out inside her head. She kept her body relaxed, legs crossed at the ankles, hugging her knees. She made herself as small as possible, a trick she'd learned from her uncle so as not to be perceived as a threat.

The minute Reed returned, the Lab perked up. He tried to get up.

"Whoa there." Reed's voice was a study in calm and it seemed to have a sedating effect on the dog. Walking over, Reed bent down and put his hand out for the Lab to sniff.

Instead, the pup put his head in Reed's hand, and it melted Addison's heart.

"I think you found yourself a dog," she said to Reed.

"Give him some time. He probably just smells all the other animals on me. He'll come around and there's no way I'm taking your dog from you."

"Looks like he made his choice." Who was she to argue with what the dog wanted? She was the one, after all, who'd hit him with her car.

"Don't give up on him so easily." Reed smiled at her and a dozen butterflies released in her chest.

She didn't respond because she couldn't pick from the several thoughts that crowded her head. Things like, she wasn't as good with animals as he was, and, she didn't have time for him and he must realize it, raised to the surface. There were too many others to get into a mental debate with herself.

Plus, what did she have to offer the animal? Maybe he knew on instinct that Reed would be a better dog dad. She lived in the city and worked long hours. Reed was part owner of a ranch. The family had more acreage than the fictional Ewings on the popular TV show in the seventies set in the city of the same name.

On the other hand, Reed had more acreage than anyone could count. There were animals all over the place with more pets than people. The Lab would have room to roam and plenty of cohorts.

"It's fine," she said, and she needed to change the subject to one that didn't leave a hole in her heart. It was silly, really, because she barely knew the animal and yet his rejection stung. "It was really great of the others to show up on such short notice. Talk about the cavalry arriving."

Reed caught her gaze and held it. She tried to ignore how locking gazes with him made her heart pound her ribs. The thought of the couple of kisses they'd shared popped into her thoughts, causing heat to crawl up her neck.

"It meant a lot that Levi came. Things have been tense between us ever since his father had an accident in the equipment room at the ranch that left him in a coma. My father was in the room at the time but claims he didn't see or hear anything."

"And? Do you believe him?" She cocked her head to one side.

"Families are complicated, aren't they?"

She issued a sharp sigh. "Truer words have never been spoken."

10

"What do you think happened?"

Reed thought about Addison's question for several long moments. The debate in his mind, the torment, was that he hadn't told a soul about his visit to the sheriff's office. Granted, everyone had been called in to give a statement considering the incident happened on the property. And he'd never wanted to talk about what had transpired in her office until now, until Addison. It was like a weight had been docked on his chest for weeks now, making it almost impossible to breathe. And here in front of him sat a chance to lift some of the burden.

"To be honest, I have no idea. If you're asking me if I think my dad is guilty, I have no clue about that either. How messed up is that? Because I want to believe he is incapable of trying to kill the man he didn't have a problem leaving me and my brothers with after our mother died." At some point during his speech, Addison moved to his side. She had her hand on his leg as he sat there. "How's that for a messed up family?"

"One that also loves each other deeply."

He could concede the point.

"My father confessed that he wanted to take over the family business. He asked me to join him before all this happened. I refused. Of course. There's no way I'd turn my back on the man who raised me. But, what if my dad seized an opportunity? What if I'm the reason he's in jail? Because I had to be honest with the sheriff."

"Have you spoken to him since his arrest?"

He shook his head.

"I could go with you if you wanted to talk to him."

"The offer is appreciated. It is. But that's something I need to do alone." This was more than he'd said to anyone about the situation. Some of the weight he'd been carrying lifted. He felt like he could almost breathe again. But this was as far as he could go with anyone. It was time to change the subject and refocus because the air in the room was getting a little too thin. "And we're here to talk about how I can help you, not the other way around."

Addison didn't lift her gaze to meet his and she didn't speak right away. Her hand found his. Her creamy soft skin a contrast to his that was rough from hard work.

"I hate that you're going through this, Reed. And I like it even less that you're going through it alone. I'm sure it took a lot to tell me what you did and I hope you'll trust me with more in the future. What you've told me is a lot to bear on your own. It is." With that, she brought his hand up to her lips and then pressed a tender kiss to it.

And maybe he would be able to. He was done for now. Plus, he meant the part about being there to help her.

"Finding your cousin is important to you. Right?"

"It is. I need to know what happened to her. Is she out there somewhere? Alive? Not? As much drama as my mother causes me and as much as I'd very much like her to disappear on some days, I would want to know if something happened to her. I don't care what our relationship had become. I would need to know if that makes any sense."

"Sure does. I'd like to help but I have no experience growing up in a house full of girls. I wouldn't know the first thing about how a teenaged girl thinks."

"Well, we like to keep our thoughts to ourselves." She looked up at him with a spark in her eyes. "And that mostly means writing them down in a diary. My cousin used to keep hers in her room." She pushed to standing.

The pup had gone to sleep in Reed's opposite hand. He eased it out from underneath the Lab. Then, he quietly stood and replaced the pen. For a man his size, he moved with athletic grace.

Addison pointed upstairs. Her cousin kept her diary in a box under a floorboard in the closet. It was the perfect hiding spot in an old house and the joints never quite seemed to match up in this one, leaving gaps mainly in the closets where no one walked and they could be hidden with carpet.

She led him into her cousin's room, something she'd avoided earlier in the cleaning process, figuring facing that beast would take a minute. But if Ivy's diary was still here, there might be answers. And, no, her parents wouldn't have been privileged to this information.

Addison moved to the closet and bent down on all fours. Many of Ivy's clothes still hung inside. Her room had been perfectly preserved from what Addison remembered of it. A canopy bed, full size. A matching double dresser with mirror. Same thing with the nightstand. Fairy lights that cast the room in a pink hue when turned on. So many warm memories in this room.

She reached around for the corner of the small closet.

Older homes did not come with huge closets. This one was
the size of most people's coat closets, so it wasn't a far reach.
She found the loose piece of carpet and pulled it back. The
box was there, just like she hoped it would be. She pulled it
out, the decoupage such a throwback considering they'd
made one for Ivy and one for Addison the summer after
sixth grade.

The box was heavy enough. She opened it to find a
couple of small diaries.

"Not sure which one is the most recent." She pulled the
top one out and then handed the box to Reed. "These all
have locks. I'm pretty certain it won't be difficult to bust
them, though."

He took the offering and selected the next journal. In
total, there were four journals of varying sizes. None bigger
than a five-by-seven picture frame. Addison tried to open
the one in her hand. She realized the key was tucked inside
the spine. That was easy. Reed already had a pocket knife
out, jiggering the one in his hand open. They both met with
quick success.

She scanned the entries. It didn't take long to realize this
diary was from seventh grade. "Mine is old. How did
you do?"

"Not much better." He held the book open to reveal
drawings of butterflies and rainbows. He flipped the pages.
"She couldn't have been much more than grade school
when she used this journal."

Addison felt her shoulders slump forward as she
checked the other two with the same luck. "I guess she
would have her diary with her when she left."

"Makes sense that she wouldn't leave it behind if she ran
away."

"I guess. Some of her clothes are gone. I wish my aunt

was still here so I could ask her if she cleaned out Ivy's closet or if my cousin packed up her belongings."

"Did she have a car when she turned sixteen?"

Addison shook her head. "We were both bummed that our parents had no intention of handing over the keys to a vehicle when we had our magic birthdays. My uncle had an old truck he said she could use whenever she 'needed' to go somewhere."

"Sounds about right. In a town like this one, there's an abundance of old pickup trucks. I've overheard parents of teenage drivers talk about the benefits of a vehicle not having a backseat, thinking no good could come from pilling a bunch of teenagers into one small space with wheels and an engine."

"We used to sit in the back and sometimes on the hood of vehicles at your ranch if I'm remembering correctly."

"And drive on the back roads that now lead to our separate homes." He rocked his head. "I do remember. We got in serious trouble with Miss Penny if we got caught."

"Kids can do some seriously stupid stuff."

"Yep. You won't hear me deny it." He chuckled and it was a low rumble in his chest that was both sexy and endearing. It also stirred feelings in her chest that she didn't have time to think about. Plus, he'd opened up earlier and then a wall had come up between them.

"Brains aren't fully developed, I guess." She shrugged.

"In my experience, grown people can pull some pretty idiotic moves." He didn't mention his father specifically, but they both knew he was talking about him.

Her mind immediately snapped to her mother and Benjamin. "I can attest to that."

"All is not lost. The sheriff should be getting back to us. She might have already texted about a file on Ivy. Your aunt and uncle would have filed a missing person's report. They might have given statements. It'll give us a better sense of what timeline we're working with other than the year in general."

He was trying to give her a boost of hope and that must mean the expression on her face was defeated.

"The last thing I remember about her was how much she loved being here. Then," she snapped her fingers, "poof. It's like she became a whole new person."

"Teenagers can have personality changes. As much as I like to think we were all saints, I know for certain that we were far from it."

"You guys were amazing. You couldn't ask to be part of a better family to hear Ivy tell it."

"We were once. I don't know how the dynamics will change once the truth gets out."

"The truth. That's all I want. Why is it so hard to find?"

"Good question." Reed's lips compressed into a thin line. "How about we make a deal?"

She stretched out her legs because her feet were going to sleep.

"Okay..." She drew out the word.

"No lies between us. In here, we tell the truth to each other."

"Which doesn't mean we have to talk about things we aren't ready to speak about," she insisted. "We take our time and only share what we're comfortable with."

REED HAD to stop himself from leaning forward and claiming that mouth of hers. He had to fight every instinct inside his body, every muscle that made him want to reach out to her and then haul her in his arms. He'd tell himself that he would be doing it for her benefit. To provide a shoulder to lean on and a temporary shelter to a storm. But, the honest to God's truth was that he needed her as much as he sensed she needed him.

His secret from his family was eating away at him. Could he tell Levi? With a six-month age difference between them, the two had always been close to the point he was closer to Levi than his siblings. And yet, coming clean about his father and what he told the sheriff, then holding the information in, felt like the worst betrayal to everyone important to him.

Not confiding in Levi was half the reason a truck was docked on his chest and guilt ate away at him from the inside out.

Addison slowly flipped through Ivy's diary pages. "I thought for certain we'd find something in one of these."

"Like I said earlier, she most likely took her most recent one with her when she left," he surmised.

"She didn't even take all her clothes." Addison exhaled a slow breath before pinching the bridge of her nose like she was staving off a headache. She stood up and turned around. The closet was behind her, door open. She sifted through the outfits. "Some of her favorites are still here."

"How long has it been since the last time you saw her?"

"Gosh, I'd have to think about it for a second." She compressed her lips and her eyes unfocused, like she was looking inside herself for the answer. "It's been too many years to remember."

"I'd imagine teenage girls' taste changes quite a bit every year," he pointed out.

"Especially at that age," she agreed. "I can remember a phase where everything she wore was black. She thought it highlighted her blonde hair." She laughed and the sound was musical. "Then, there was the fuzzy sweater phase. Oh my word, even with how hot it gets in Texas, she had on a sweater and some of them were crop-topped. What was the point of that?"

"I remember girls wearing those in school with jeans hiked up to their fourth rib so they weren't in dress code violation."

"Yes. Then there was the trend of layering shorts over leggings."

"Oh, those were lookers," he teased. "We had mono-chrome sports jerseys to look forward to."

"I remember those. As I recall, those were unisex." She rocked her head and pretended to flip up her collar. "We thought we were so stylin' in those jerseys."

"I much prefer jeans, T-shirt, and boots."

"They look good on you too." Her cheeks flushed again and she quickly turned around to face the closet.

Reed should probably address the elephant in the room —the attraction simmering between them. Clearly, he wasn't so great at the whole talking out his feelings thing, despite the fact he'd apparently told her more than any other person about his situation with his family.

"I better go check on the Lab." He pushed up to standing. "Any idea what you plan to name him?"

"You change your mind about that?"

"What?"

"Don't you remember advising me against giving him a name when we were at the vet's office?"

"Right. That. You know, I can be a real jerk sometimes. I just didn't want you to get too attached and then have someone show up to claim him. Thought it might break your heart. Not giving him a name would help you keep a distance from him." He shook his head. "But that dog is yours. No one has called around in search of him, which leads me to believe he doesn't belong to anyone in this community or anyone who pit-stopped here or was driving through. A responsible pet owner would have called every vet's office and probably the sheriff too."

"Problem is, he likes you more than he does me."

"I smell like a ranch. What dog wouldn't love that? Doesn't mean he won't bond with you," he pointed out.

"We'll see."

"Maybe you should come with me," he said.

"Nah. I want to stay up here for a few more minutes." There was a wistful quality to her tone that made him want to march right back in the room and sit with her. Something told him she'd be reliving memories—memories that would hurt now that Ivy was gone.

"Do you want me to stick around?"

She shook her head.

Walking out of the room and then down the stairs caused his chest to squeeze. Leaving her alone when she was clearly upset went against every fiber in his being. Strange how deeply invested he'd become in her happiness.

11

"Look what I found."

Reed was on the floor with the pup when Addison bounded into the living room. She was holding out a piece of paper that had been balled up.

"Where'd you find that?"

"Underneath her nightstand, kind of wedged behind the bed." She crossed the room and sat down beside him. He ignored the heat ricocheting between them and watched as she smoothed the page against her thigh.

"And?"

"It's not her handwriting. I can tell you that much."

"A guy's?" The scribbles looked like a guy's handwriting to Reed.

"I think so. It says, 'I'm sorry about last night. I didn't mean for that to happen again. I just get so mad sometimes. Meet me?'" Addison blinked up at him. "This reads like she was in an abusive relationship."

"Makes sense. The first thing an abuser does is isolate the object of his affection from family members."

"That would explain why she stopped talking to her

parents and the later disappearance." Addison fisted her hands. "She might have even wanted to come home, but he wouldn't allow it."

"And since she left of her own will, there might not have been anything the sheriff could have done at the time, even if Skinner had been first-rate."

It was getting late. Night had descended around them. Addison bit back a yawn.

"We can regroup in the morning when our minds are fresh," he said, thinking she'd been through quite a bit for one day.

"This day has been one of the longest of my life." She set the note in between them. "We'll get my aunt's laptop tomorrow morning and possibly more information from Laney."

"I'll take the couch."

"Be serious. That looks way too small for you," she countered.

"Nah. I won't need more than a few minutes of shuteye here and there. There are times when I go two or three days without much more than catnaps throughout the day if I'm tracking poachers or searching for a lost heifer. I'll most likely nod off at some point."

"Are you one hundred percent certain?" she asked.

"A thousand percent. Believe me when I say ranchers don't generally sleep a whole lot, especially during calving season, which we're thankfully not in right now. I don't get off the property much when that happens."

"Will you tell me why in the morning?" She bit back another yawn.

"Yes. Get some sleep. I'll be right here when you wake up."

She scooted over to the sleeping pup, leaned in, and then whispered, "Hero."

A good name for a good dog. And he was glad that she didn't listen to his comment in Derek's office about not giving the guy a name. Hero deserved to be named.

She stood up, and paused. "Are you sure you'll be okay down here?"

"Peachy."

"Okay." She said on a sigh before leaving the room. He heard the stairs creak and groan as she climbed up them. He figured he needed to get settled in, so he took off his belt and toed off his boots. He set both on the side of the couch. His Stetson was already there. It had been removed for the cleaning job. Miss Penny had taught him well, despite cleaning up for him most of his life. He kept his own house clean on the ranch, with the help of the cleaner she sent every other week to do some of the heavy lifting, like bathrooms and scrubbing floors. His work on the ranch left him too tired most days to tackle those jobs. But he kept up after himself like he figured every grown adult should know how to do.

The stairs creaked and groaned as he heard Addison descend. His first glimpse of her in her oversized T-shirt, and it didn't look like much else, stirred more than his heart. Her arms were full with a blanket, pillow, and sheets.

"I figure the only way Hero will get used to me is if I sleep down here beside him. So, you're welcome to take a proper bed upstairs. Either my cousin's or my aunt and uncle's. I'm good down here with my dog." She had the most adorable pout when she was tired.

"You take the couch, I'll take the floor." He started to get up.

"No. No. No. I'm on the floor. I want him to wake up to me." She waved her hands like she was stopping a speeding car.

"Okay. Set your stuff down and do me a favor." He would let her win this one. He almost laughed out loud at his word choice. He highly doubted he'd *let* her do anything. She was strong enough to be an equal match, and it made her even more desirable in his eyes.

"Anything. Name it."

"Go upstairs and get the shirt you had on earlier." His request was met with a look. In fact, she shot him a look like he had four chins.

"Trust me?" he asked.

She kept an eyebrow raised but she did, in fact, run back upstairs and retrieve her shirt. She held it out. "What do you plan to do—"

His actions stopped her midsentence as he folded the shirt and placed it next to Hero's head. "That way, he'll get more comfortable with your scent. He'll start to recognize it and feel calmer around you."

"Oh. That's a cool trick." She looked impressed and that made his heart sing more than he wanted to admit.

"And, by the way, you look amazing in anything you wear. I've never seen someone look sexier in a T-shirt."

His comment made her smile. Good. She should know that she was a beautiful person inside and out. Her kind heart touched him in a deep place. Her determination to get Hero to like her and to stick by his side even when he was still so nervous around her was an admirable trait. Don't even get him started on the fact she was trying to save her father's legacy and honor the man long after his death.

Reed didn't want to think about more of her good qualities—and there were a lot. Geography aside, as well as their very different lives, she was exactly the kind of person he could see himself wanting to get to know better. A lot of good the realization did. He would never think of asking her to give up her family legacy any more than he could give up his. He just wasn't built that way and, based on what he knew of her already, neither was she.

"Goodnight, Reed." Her sexy, sleepy voice cracked more of the casing around his heart as he turned off the light.

"Night."

A SOUND CAUSED Addison to sit straight up. Her back ached from sleeping on the floor despite making her spot as comfortable as humanly possible. Hero was gone. A glance at the sofa said Reed was missing. She scrambled to her feet and shoved her hair off her face. She'd placed a rubber band around her wrist, so she grabbed it and secured her hair in a ponytail.

The smell of coffee wafted through the room and the sound she'd heard, she realized, came from the kitchen. The sun was up. She checked her phone on the coffee table. It was a quarter after seven. There were also no less than half a dozen text messages, none of which she wanted to deal with before coffee.

She hurried into the kitchen to find a shirtless Reed standing at the stove heating something that smelled amazing. He moved with athletic grace and her heart freefell at the sight of his muscled back.

Hero was curled up underneath the table on the blanket from last night. Her shirt was tucked under his head as a makeshift pillow.

"Morning," she said, not wanting to startle Reed as he worked.

"Hey." When he turned and smiled, her legs turned to rubber.

"Coffee," was all she could manage to croak. She moved to the pot and fixed a cup, pouring a little milk in. Next, she moved to the kitchen table. Instead of sitting in a chair, she took a seat on the floor. Rather than put any pressure on Hero to accept her, she sat with her side to him so he wouldn't feel threatened by her presence. Yesterday had been such a runaway train, she hadn't thought about how vulnerable he must have been feeling. In some small way, she hoped he realized they were there to help.

Hero watched her movements with weary eyes. It was okay. No pressure. He'd come around or he wouldn't. She would take care of him either way.

"How'd you sleep?" Reed asked.

"Uncomfortably." She rolled her shoulders, trying to work out some of the kinks. "I think I dreamed about Ivy. We were so young and naïve. Neither one of us had a lot of dating experience. She had such a hard crush on you. I used to call her boy crazy."

"Well, she has good taste in men," he teased.

"Can't fault her there," she quipped. And she couldn't. Reed had always been the McGannon Addison would have liked if her cousin hadn't already claimed him. "I just keep thinking that her inexperience could have made her easier to manipulate. You know?"

"It's possible."

"I wish he'd signed the note. Then we'd know who he was. As it is, we aren't any closer to finding her."

"If she is the one who broke into the house, maybe she's

stalking your social media page. If she knew you were here, she might show up."

"That's a really great point. Maybe we can take a picture of me on the porch. Or next to the barn. Some place she will recognize and have to know I'm here."

"It's worth a try." He had two plates in his hands when he turned around. "Breakfast first?"

"It smells amazing." And they were making progress. Baby steps but she would take what she could get and run with it.

Surprisingly, Addison cleared her plate in a matter of minutes. She saved a scrap of bacon, placing it on the flat of her palm and sticking her hand as close to Hero as she felt comfortable doing.

He leaned his head toward her and licked the bacon off her hand. His warm tongue tickled her palm. He took the bacon gently, and that was another sign of hope.

"How's he doing this morning?" She motioned toward him.

"Better. He was able to walk outside on his own and relieve himself. He ate breakfast and had some water. I gave him medicine because I didn't want to wake you."

Again, she'd have to get used to being around someone as capable as Reed. Living with her mother, which thankfully she no longer did, as her caregiver had made her used to caring for others with no expectation of help in return.

"Thank you. For breakfast and..." Before she could finish her sentence a surprising tear sprang to her eyes. She took a second before finishing so she could get hold of herself. "It's just really nice of you to do everything you've done and it means a lot to me."

"My pleasure." The tone in his voice said he meant it.

"It's probably going to surprise you being from the city, but this is what we do in small towns. We have each other's backs. It's just being friendly and it's not as big of a deal as you're making it out to be. I don't deserve to be thanked for doing what comes natural."

"Not enough people feel the same way as you do. Where I'm from, people look out for themselves. It's just the way in Dallas. We all stick to our own business and leave each other alone."

"Sounds lonely if you ask me," he muttered. And, damned if he wasn't right.

She picked up her empty plate and his.

He put a hand up to stop her, but she cautioned him with a look.

"You cooked. I clean. Period. No one does all the jobs. Not even at the deli." Her admonishment netted another smile.

Reed took a sip of his coffee.

"Go ahead. I'll sit back and enjoy my fresh brew." He crossed his legs at the ankles and leaned back in his chair.

"How much sleep did you get last night?" she asked on her way to the sink.

"Fifteen minutes here and there."

"Oh. Did I keep you awake?"

"If you're asking if you snore, the answer is yes, but it's cute as hell."

"I do not." Her cheeks seriously flamed now. She felt the heat as it crawled up her neck.

"Sure...let's go with that," he said, laughing.

"Great." She didn't do sleepovers in relationships because she had to be at work so early in the morning. She figured it was easier to stay at her own place that was around the corner from the deli. Having someone sleep over wasn't happening because she didn't want to leave someone alone in her place. It felt...weird. And yet, being here with Reed seemed like the most natural thing.

Her heart was going to be in trouble once she wrapped up her family's affairs. The thought of going home had never made her want to cry before or felt like such a lonely proposition before. She'd never equated living alone to being lonely. She'd relished the space after her mother moved out to be with Benjamin. Speaking of which, Addison needed to check her messages after she made the social media post.

She looked up to find Reed studying her.

"What?" she asked.

"Nothing. You're beautiful when you get that crinkle in your forehead."

"You mean wrinkle."

"No, this one goes away when you relax. Wrinkles are permanent. I have a few of those working up thanks to long hours in the sun." He laughed.

"Oh, yeah, your skin is...awful." He had one of those golden, sun-kissed looks that only added to his general hotness.

He wiggled his eyebrows and that really made her laugh. It felt good and she couldn't remember the last time she had a full-belly laugh. Some of the tension she'd been carrying around since losing her father started to break apart. Wow, the realization she hadn't let up or really laughed in years struck a deep chord.

Her cell buzzed in the living room and she started to rush into the other room. The thing was normally glued to her palm or tucked inside her apron. Some of the calls and texts needed to be addressed right away.

Or did they?

Had she been living in a broken and reactive state for longer than she cared to acknowledge? The answer was a resounding, yes. If she thought about what she *wanted* instead of what she felt *compelled* to do...how different would her life be?

12

"The pic has been up on my social media account for an hour. No responses." Addison positioned her laptop toward Reed.

"She might not respond but that doesn't mean she didn't or won't see it. If she is out there somewhere and still in hiding, she definitely wouldn't say anything on a public platform."

"Did I mention how little patience I have?" She'd smoothed over the kink with the flour supplier that Benjamin had tried to cancel their standing order with, and responded to her mother's multiple texts asking for more responsibility around the deli when the cell went off in her hand. She would take this one. "Hey, Connie. What's up?"

"Sorry to call you while you're technically on leave, but I overheard Benjamin telling Harper there were going to be some big changes made around here. Am I missing something or is he talking out his backside again?" Connie was as practical as they came. She had a two-year degree from community college and one of the best work ethics Addison had ever witnessed.

"I'm not planning on any changes." Addison released a sharp sigh. "How much of a handful is he being while I'm gone?"

"He's probably not any worse. You're just not here to balance him out."

"I thought by giving him a part-time job in the business, he'd quiet down for a while."

"To hear him tell it, he's five minutes away from taking the helm." She could almost hear Connie rolling her eyes. "I'm telling everyone you'll be back soon and everything will go back to normal again."

"I need to think of a new job for him. Find a way to get him out of the deli."

"Night stocker?" Connie laughed but there was still noticeable tension in her voice.

"I was thinking maybe dishwasher," she teased.

"At least he would be *doing* something besides running his mouth."

"Sorry about that. I hope it's not too stressful." Addison had no plans to hand over the reins to Benjamin. Why did she really even give him a job in the first place? The answer came quickly. To keep an eye on him so he didn't hurt her mother.

"You know me. I'll be fine. I just wanted to double-check that you're still coming back. Not sure this place could run without you."

She didn't point out this was only her second day to be gone. Her absence wasn't off to a great start.

"I'll wrap my aunt's affairs up as fast as I can." It was a daunting thought, actually. More of that heavy sadness tried to edge its way in. "And be back. It shouldn't be too long." At least, that was the hope.

"Okay. Good. We need you around here." Connie was

being kind. She could run the place on her own without
blinking after working there for the past three years at Addison's side. Come to think of it, why hadn't Addison gone on
vacation or taken leave before now? She'd only taken a day
here and there. An afternoon spent kayaking at Lake Ray
Hubbard, where no motorized vehicles were allowed. A day
wandering around the downtown Dallas public library.
Never two days in a row, let alone a whole week.

If Addison was going to start psychoanalyzing herself,
that seemed like a good place to start.

"Don't listen to him in the meantime. If there are any
changes, they'll come through me not him. And, technically,
you're his boss in my absence, so don't put up with any
monkey business."

"You know I won't." Connie could handle herself. It's the
reason Addison felt comfortable enough to leave her in
charge.

"Call me if anything comes up. I'm just here at my aunt's
place, figuring out what to do with her things." Her voice
hitched on the last part. Addison cleared her throat. "It's
fine, though. I'm good."

"Yeah." Connie hesitated and her concern came through
the line. The two weren't exactly friends, but they did spend
so much time around each other the line between boss and
employee crossed into something that felt a lot more like
friendship. They didn't have sleepovers or sing into hairbrushes, let alone divulge deep, dark secrets, and yet they
had an appreciation for one another. A compatible working
relationship that bordered on friendship. At least, Addison
figured if they'd met under different circumstances, they
might be friends.

"I got the flour supplier straightened out. Anything else
comes up, I'm a text or phone call away."

"Right." Again, Connie hesitated. Then came, "If you ever want to talk..." Another beat of silence. "I'm here. You know my number."

"Thanks. I'll keep that in mind."

Connie's gesture was kind. More than kind, actually. It was an offering of friendship. Had Addison closed herself off to everyone around her, only focusing on the business and her mother? Her schedule left very little room for a personal life. She needed to change that.

Addison ended the call. She held the phone in her hand for a long moment, thinking how nice it would be to have a friend she confided in and vice versa. Growing up an only child hadn't given her a whole lot of experience in letting people in. It seemed as though only kids either became the life of the party or the most awkward one in the room.

Addison set her phone down on the kitchen table. She looked around for a notepad and pen, thinking she needed to start by making a list.

The back door opened, Reed walked in with Hero by his side. The dog was up and around, hobbling a bit on what had turned out to be a bruised hip. Thank heaven for small miracles.

"I just got a text from the sheriff," he started as he held the door open for Hero. "Whoever was inside here must have been wearing gloves. No prints other than yours."

"Whoever came inside knew they were breaking the law." Would Ivy? She might have gotten herself into a mess of a situation if she was thinking like a criminal. The thought didn't sit well. Had her cousin gotten mixed up with something like drugs? Something that was so bad that she would turn to breaking the law?

It was almost impossible to imagine coming from a loving home like this one had been. And yet, it was a plausible explanation for the behavior changes that would have had to take place. Granted. Ivy had never exactly been in the popular crowd. Still. This was extreme.

"Did you tell her about the note?" she asked, again realizing she likely put her fingerprints all over the evidence. The note painted her cousin in a different light. One whose self-esteem must have been at an all-time low to allow a jerk to come into her life. Based on her experience with a couple of her employees over the years, she knew intelligent young women didn't always make the best choices when it came to the opposite sex. There were those who liked the thrill of dating someone they deemed edgy. Others were charmed into relationships only to find out the old bait and switch tactic had sucked them in. They went into it thinking the guy was charming, fell for him, and then his true colors came out. For some, they hung around after, hoping to get the relationship back on solid footing. It was probably just Addison, but she was out the door at the first hint she'd bought a Mercedes and somehow came home with a tenspeed.

Somewhere in the haze of her thoughts, she saw Reed's acknowledgment. He texted back and forth a couple of minutes before requesting to see the note. He took a pic, sent it, then set his phone down.

"There isn't a file on Ivy, but there was a complaint from her parents about her disappearing. She was seventeen at the time, so there wasn't much Sheriff Skinner could do about it. That's the legal age in Texas. She could quit school, move out. If an apartment would rent to her without a parent's endorsement, so be it. She could do what she wanted."

At seventeen, Ivy could do as she pleased. Seventeen hardly seemed old enough to have life figured out. But then,

Addison had stepped into the responsibility of running the family's business when she wasn't yet that old.

"Right. I was sixteen when it happened and she's six months older than me. She would have already had her birthday."

He nodded.

"Laney would like to pick up the note and see if she can lift a print from there," he said.

"The only time I need to leave today is to go pick up my aunt and uncle's belongings from the home. Other than that, I'm here." For how long, she had no idea. The pressure from trying to run her business from out of town hit full force before she'd downed her first cup of coffee.

And before her mother's need for attention doubled.

HERO WAS MAKING GOOD PROGRESS. It had been nearly twenty-four hours since the accident and he was walking on his own. A bruised hip was nothing to take lightly. The animal's age and overall condition made healing a whole lot faster. The bite marks would take a while to heal, but they were no longer bleeding. His shyness said he'd been neglected, possibly abused, or left for dead after being dropped off in the country as some jerks thought it was okay to do.

Addison, on the other hand, didn't look to be fairing so well. She studied her cell phone as she chewed on her thumbnail. The intensity level was through the roof after he heard on a call with what had sounded like one of her employees.

"Everything okay back home?" he asked.

She blew out a breath without looking up.

"Not really. Benjamin is causing all kinds of trouble for me. I cleaned up his flour debacle but he's spreading rumors with my employees and generally stirring up unrest. I can't imagine the clean-up job I'm going to have once I get home. And I can't think straight while I'm here, which is where I need to focus my energy."

"You have a lot on your plate," he agreed.

"Sure do."

"I'm not one for making lists, but I've heard they can be good for some." He winked and it caused her heart to skip a couple of beats.

She picked up a pad of paper and a pen, held it out toward him. "Apparently, I'm not all that good at it either. I used to be. I keep getting interrupted by my mom every time I think I'm about to make progress."

"Yeah? Does she usually reach out to you this many times in a twenty-four hour period?"

"Not usually. I think it's throwing her off that I'm gone. She's been acting strange ever since my aunt died."

"How so?"

"At first she was stressed about the possibility of me leaving and now she seems like she's trying to edge me out of the family business to give her new husband something to do." She blew out a frustrated breath. "I'm probably being too harsh."

"Not from my standpoint. Sounds like you're being edged out of the business you've been running almost single-handedly since your father died." His statement hit home because it was true.

"Here I've been judging my cousin for not having boundaries with a boyfriend when I can't say that I have any with my own family. Maybe it's a genetic defect." She chewed on the thumbnail harder.

Talking about her family caused her tension levels to raise and she was about to bite off her thumbnail if they didn't change the subject soon. Something didn't sit right with her mother's actions. Reed chalked it up to the fact he hadn't grown up with one. He had Miss Penny and she'd been the best surrogate parent a person could ask for. It was Miss Penny who picked him up after practice and made sure he had on a clean shirt when he went to school. She fixed countless meals, making sure everyone had all the required nutrients the doctor recommended growing boys get. She did his laundry until she trusted him enough with the machines to let him do his own. And she was the one who sat with him at the doctor's office when his temperature soared to a hundred and four the year he got the flu. She was always there for him if he needed anything and he couldn't remember a time when she wasn't taking care of him. If he'd been a talker, she was the type of person who would have sat up all night and listened if that was what it took.

He'd always heard about the special relationship between a mother and daughter. Couldn't draw on personal experience considering both his father and uncle had all boys.

"Your genetics are better than most," he said and that got her to look up and smile.

"My mom has so many needs." She exhaled and her shoulders rounded forward. "I can't say we're very close. She has needs. I do whatever I can to meet them and make sure she's happy."

"Who looks out for your needs?"

"Me."

"You're very capable of taking care of yourself." He admired her independence. She was just feisty enough to take on the world. He couldn't help but notice that she gave to others until she had nothing left for herself. "So, don't take this the wrong way."

An eyebrow shot up.

"You deserve to have someone in your life who looks out for you. Friend. Boyfriend. Significant other. An 'it's complicated' relationship."

"Well then someone needs to add a few hours into the day because, honestly, relationships exhaust me more than anything else and I don't have time to baby someone, take care of my mother, run a business and…"

She stopped right there and he hoped she heard how that sounded.

Addison put her hands up in the surrender position. "I think it's been easier to take care of everyone else and ignore my own needs. Maybe then I wouldn't have to deal with how lonely my life is."

It was most likely the broken part of him that connected so well with the broken part of her. In that moment, he knew exactly how she felt. Busy but empty.

"Maybe the time you've been given to take care of your aunt and uncle's affairs will give you a minute to step out of your normal life and think about what you want for a change instead of keeping yourself busy with everything other people need." He was being real prophetic here. "And to be fair, I have to say this goes for me too. The crazy thing about filling up your life with 'busy' makes it easy to ignore some of the stuff that matters."

She was rocking her head in agreement. "I don't want to wake up in forty years regretting my whole existence. You know?"

"Yes. I guess I never slowed down long enough to face it.

I know I'll never regret living in Texas and working the land. Being part of my family's legacy gives me a purpose."

"I understand that."

Of course she would. The two of them had more similarities than he'd first realized. And the pull to kiss her was stronger than a hundred and ten mile an hour wind in a hurricane.

Would Reed regret reclaiming those cherry lips of hers? Because a growing part of him wanted to do just that—and an overwhelming second was that he wanted more than one night or a couple of days with her.

13

A n urge to kiss Reed was a tsunami building inside Addison. This time, she would be strong and not act on impulse like she had the other couple of times she'd pushed up to her tiptoes and pressed a kiss to those gorgeous thick lips of his.

Especially since looking into those dark eyes of his was intoxicating and caused her to want to go for it again without caring about the consequences. The only thing stopping her was the all-too-real reminder of the pain headed her way when she walked out of Cattle Cove and his life forever.

Crazy that she'd considered asking if he was up for trying a long-distance thing once she left, which was presumptive. Yes, their chemistry sizzled off the charts. But that didn't mean there was anything long-lasting going on despite the fact what was going on between them was different than anything she'd ever experienced before.

Had no one been worth the effort in the past?

She'd dated decent people. Right? Her brain wanted to argue no one was this special. And that was probably true.

Reed had that rare mix of drop-dead gorgeous looks with a casual attitude that said he didn't think he was God's gift to women. Normally, a guy with a chiseled jawline like his and a face of hard angles and planes knew exactly what he was working with. Not Reed. If he did, he obviously didn't care. Maybe care was the wrong word. He didn't place all his self-worth from what stared back at him in the mirror.

Don't even get her started on most rich guys she'd been around. A few came into the deli and she'd gone out with a couple of them over the years. They never lasted. She never wanted a second date with someone who cared more about where he parked his sports car than her. She didn't need to be the center of attention, but she didn't want to take a back-seat to a Porsche either.

Plus, she just wasn't the sports car type. She never understood the appeal of sitting so low to the ground or feeling every bump on the road. The only part she understood about driving a sports car was the zippy engine.

"Your forehead is creasing again. That usually means you're concentrating on something you don't like."

She laughed. Reed knew her better in the short time they'd spent together than half the men she dated for months. She chalked it up to him being observant in general and not specifically into her.

"Yeah? I was just thinking about a couple of my exes," she confessed.

He bristled, making a show of disdain. It was over-the-top and made her laugh.

"Yep. That about sums it up," she teased. And since she figured a change of subject was in order, she said, "I should probably head over to pick up my aunt and uncle's things."

"My truck is right outside," he offered.

"I'm ready to go whenever you are," she said.

"Let's roll."

She glanced at Hero. "Think he's able to come with us?"

"I don't see why not. He probably won't like being here alone." He motioned toward her feet. "And he's already warming up to you."

At some point during their conversation, Hero had spread out. His head was now the closest to her foot he'd willingly been since this whole ordeal started. Progress.

"I noticed." She smiled as she stood up. "Come on, Hero."

Addison picked up her cell, figuring she needed to address Connie's comments about her mother's husband. She sent a quick text. *Not planning any major changes at the deli. Please make sure your husband knows.*

Hero stood up and followed her into the living room where she retrieved her purse. While her cell was still in her hand, it started vibrating. She figured her mom wasn't happy and decided to let it sit instead of responding. That meant not looking at her phone because she'd be too tempted to respond.

The thing started going crazy. By the time she reached Reed's truck and helped Hero inside, the buzzing didn't stop.

This was a bit much, even for her mother.

"Everything okay?" Reed asked as he started the engine and put the gearshift in reverse.

"I basically asked my mom to tell her husband to chill out until I get back. This is the response I'm getting." She checked her messages. The texts might be coming from her mother's inbox but there was no way she was the one writing them. *Spoilt brat.* That was one of the less angry ones.

"Doesn't sound good."

"Nope." Rather than continue reading, she deleted the thread.

"Might be better to give him a minute to cool off."

"I just deleted them." Her fuse was shrinking. "I can't believe the audacity of him to think it's okay to talk to me like that for one. And for another, he's the one going around spreading rumors with *my* employees."

"What's he saying?" The concern in his voice was evident.

"He's telling them big changes are coming to the deli. To be clear, he shouldn't be addressing *my* employees with any authority. Not to mention the fact the only change that's now on my agenda is him." She figured waiting until she returned would be best. "This helps me make the decision to keep him far away from my father's business. My mom isn't welcome anymore, either. It's time to cut the cord with those two. She made a decision to spend the rest of her life with him. I didn't."

"True. I know all about family tensions and how quickly they can bubble over," he admitted.

"How are you handling yours?"

He laughed. "I'm here, aren't I?"

It was funny and obviously meant to be a joke, but one that stung her pride. Call her crazy, but she was hoping he was still there to be near her. And her chest shouldn't deflate when she was reminded he wasn't, even though it did.

REED PULLED up in front of Graceful Acres's main building. Addison had been quiet on the ride over. The texts from her stepfather had set her into a sour mood, as they would anyone. Frustration was still coming off her in waves.

Families were complicated as hell.

He was a family-oriented person, so his non-relationship with his father bit twice as hard. All it would have taken was a little effort on the old man's part for Reed to give him more of a chance. What had he done instead? Tried to hatch a plan to bite the hand that fed him when he was down on his luck. How was that for gratitude?

Not to mention the obvious...his father might have tried to kill his brother. So, yeah, he understood complicated families as much as anyone could. To prove the higher power had a sense of humor—if there was one—McGannons were built to have each other's backs. It was ingrained in their DNA. So, it went against nature for them to be at odds. The one person Reed would normally go to wasn't an option either. How would he bring up the topic of his father with his uncle?

"I'll check in with the receptionist and see what we need to do," Addison said. She eased out of the truck, making no quick movements around Hero.

"I'll be right here when you get back." He forced a smile.

She looked at him with those beautiful eyes and then took in a deep breath. She cocked her head to one side and then said, "Here goes nothing."

Instead of speaking empty encouragement, he reached over to her hand that was resting on the passenger seat, giving it a caress. In that moment, words weren't necessary.

She nodded and then took off toward the double glass doors. He waited with Hero. "You got yourself a real good home with her. I hope you realize how lucky you are."

A growing part of him wanted to figure out a way to keep the lines open once she handled her relative's affairs. Could they keep in touch? Try to the long-distance thing? Because the prospect of going on a date with someone who wasn't

Addison suddenly held little appeal. Which was crazy, right? They'd barely gotten to know each other despite feeling like he'd known her for his entire life. It was a foreign thought to someone who didn't usually spend time with anyone he hadn't known most of his life.

But then, his father's situation made him rethink what he knew about people. They only let others in so far, only showing what they wanted to be visible. There was the view from the outside and then the real person who lurked beneath the surface. Manners and decorum taught people to hide their true thoughts and opinions from the world.

It was the eyes that usually told the real story and that was another thing bugging Reed about his father. Any time he looked into the man's eyes, he saw greed. His father had proposed taking a legal route even though his eyes showed desperation.

Addison came out of the double doors not five minutes after she went inside. She tucked her chin to her chest and looked to the side. He tightened his grip on the steering wheel and faced forward.

She opened the door and cleared her throat. "We have to meet a maintenance guy around back. He'll load up their belongings."

"Okay." He gave her privacy as she reclaimed her seat next to Hero. Out of the corner of his eye, he saw the dog put his head in her lap after she clicked her seatbelt on, and he'd be damned if his own eyes weren't beginning to well up.

He drove around to the back of the building in companionable silence. The maintenance worker waited out back with a pair of wingback chairs and a chest. There were half a dozen extra-large boxes.

Reed parked but kept the vehicle running. He hopped

out of the driver's seat and opened the truck bed before helping the worker load the truck. The man who had a nametag sewed into his blue shirt that read, *Elton*, handed over a quilted bag around the size of a laptop last.

"I believe this was their only computer. Phone's inside there," he pointed, "in the pocket Mrs. Murray sewed. She was proud of that bag." She'd done a great job with the soft pink and lavender floral print.

"Thank you, Elton. I'll be sure to take good care with it." Reed reached into his pocket and pulled out a couple of twenties after shouldering the bag. He discreetly placed the money inside the flat of Elton's palm as the two shook hands.

"Thank you, sir."

Reed nodded, and then was back in the driver's seat not much more than five minutes after he'd parked. He set the bag on the floorboard in the middle. "Your aunt was partial to the bag she made."

"Those are...*were*...her favorite colors."

He put the gearshift into drive and pulled away from Graceful Acres. Elton stood there, waving. He was a decent person and one who seemed to care a lot about the residents. Strange how much those things mattered a little more in a time like this.

"I'm no expert on quilting or bags but she did a nice job on it."

"Thank you, Reed. I appreciate you coming here and helping me with her and my uncle's belongings. It's strange to think they're no longer here and the sadness of that hits me square in the chest sometimes. Like I can't breathe." She paused long enough to extend her hand over to touch his arm. "I can't imagine going through all this alone."

"This is exactly where I want to be." His words seemed to put her at ease.

Half an hour later, he pulled up to the Murray's home. As they pulled in, he realized the front door was ajar.

"Hold on. Stay here in the truck with Hero." He reached behind him and located the hunting rifle he had in a special rack behind the seat. He loaded it. "How comfortable are you with a gun?"

"I'm from Texas, aren't I?"

"Good. I'll keep the truck running. Lock the door as soon as I get out. He pulled his cell phone out. "Call your number."

She did and he heard her phone make noise from her handbag. She pulled it out and answered.

"Now, we're connected." The next gun he pulled out was from his glove box. A pistol he used out on the ranch in case he ran into coyotes or wild hogs. He cocked it, and then ran his thumb over the safety. He put the call on speaker and instructed her to do the same. Gun in one hand, phone in the other, he exited the vehicle and moved to the front porch.

"Looks like someone took a crowbar to the door," he said quietly into the receiver, leading with the barrel of his pistol.

He made an immediate left and checked the room. "Living room is clear."

The wood floor groaned underneath his weight in the hallway. He made a mental note to have that fixed. He cleared the hallway and the closet underneath the stairs. He moved to the back of the house. "Kitchen's clear and so is the laundry room."

That basically left the upstairs. He checked the powder room at the base of the stairs. Clear. Then, moved up the stairs. His mind was on high alert as he listened for any signs of an intruder. One by one, he took the stairs, figuring his biggest threat would be someone standing at the top of the landing. The hallway had two bedrooms with a bathroom in between. He'd be most vulnerable as he crested the stairwell. Back against the wall, he moved quietly and precisely.

The stairs gave him away no matter how much he tried to be stealthy. If someone was at the top, they had the advantage of being able to hear him. Beyond that, he would be back in the driver's seat.

There was no use putting off the inevitable. He stopped and listened for any sounds of breathing. When he didn't hear anything, he bum-rushed the landing, leading with his weapon. There was no sign of anyone on either side of the hallway. The bathroom was straight ahead of him. He cleared it first. Next, he moved into Ivy's bedroom checking under the bed and in the closet. Her parents' room was the last stop.

"So far, so good," he whispered into the receiver. There was no one behind him, so the only option would be in front. The realization made him truly exhale for the first time since entering the house. He took the bedroom one step at a time. Again, the wood flooring groaned, giving away his position.

Reed stopped and listened. There were times that called for rushing and times that called for retreat. This wasn't a time to rush. Inching forward, he slowly opened the door with his left elbow, keeping his phone firmly planted in one hand and his gun the other.

A sweep of the room came out okay. He moved to the closet and stood, back against the wall, next to the door instead of straight on. He gripped the handle and froze. When there was no movement, he slowly turned the ornate glass. A quick open followed by him bathing the small room in light didn't reveal any unwanted guests. He dropped down to his knees and turned to face the small enclosure. His heart pounded as he cleared the last room.

If someone had been inside the house, the flooring would have given away any advantage he might have gained by being quiet. Not this time. Fortunately, it was safe. "All clear."

He pushed up to standing and made his way down the short hallway and then the stairs. Seeing Addison in the truck, safe, was the next time he was able to release the breath he'd been holding.

Knowing she was safe meant a whole lot more to him than he wanted to analyze. All he wanted to think about for the time being was the fact she was in his truck, unharmed. The second thought was that the house could use an alarm system as he pulled out his phone and texted the sheriff.

"Again?" Sheriff Justice's response came in record time.

"Yes."

"I'm on my way. I have news."

14

Addison hopped out of the truck the minute she saw Reed. She ran into his arms and kissed him. She acted on pure instinct and didn't care about the consequences. He kissed her back. Hard. Needy. And with the kind of passion that had been missing in every kiss before him.

By the time their lips parted, her legs were rubber bands and her heart had melted.

"Thank heaven you're okay." She searched his eyes, those beautiful eyes of his, and her ribs took a beating. She'd had the call with him open and then the keypad of her phone with 9-1-1 already up and ready to go. All she would have had to do was hit send.

"I didn't touch anything. If there's a print, Sheriff Justice will be able to pick it up this time."

"What are the odds there's a print? The person was smart enough to wear gloves or wipe off the knobs before."

"True. But this time, they used a crowbar to open the front door. They were much more discreet last time."

"Speaking of the sheriff, I should—"

"She's on her way."

"Okay. Good. In the meantime, I guess we should," Addison glanced around, looking for a place to play around with the laptop, "maybe stay in the truck and see what we can find on Aunt Kay's tech."

"Right. I already interfered enough with the crime scene. Don't want to do any more damage."

Addison linked their fingers as she walked to the truck. He deposited her on the passenger side before taking the driver's seat. She ran her fingers along the quilted laptop bag, thinking how much joy her aunt always got from craft projects like this. The woman was a genius with scrap material. She'd made Addison a blanket from all the summer T-shirts she forgot to pack. Even as a small child, Addison seemed to want to leave something behind at her aunt and uncle's house to give her a reason to return. Not that she needed one on their part.

She picked up the bag and pulled out the laptop, noticing a flip phone was tucked in an inside pocket. That was a trip down memory lane. She pulled out the phone and held it in the flat of her palm. "I can't remember the last time I saw one of these."

"Whoa. Same." He smiled and she figured he was trying to ease some of her tension. "Might want to hang onto that for the Smithsonian."

"Seriously. I mean, I didn't expect my aunt and uncle to be high tech but I thought they at least might own a newer smartphone."

"Based on my not so vast experience with people over a certain age, they figure out a piece of tech and stick with it preferring to get it fixed rather than learn something unfamiliar. To be fair, tech moves fast. My phone would be considered ancient by most sixteen-year-olds' standards."

"Well, they'd have a field day with this gem." She opened it. Much to her surprise, it was charged and ready to go. "You want to see what you can find off this while I check the laptop?"

"I'll see what I can do. No promises." He took the offering and she ignored the fissions of heat from contact.

Next, she pulled out the laptop. It, too, had seen better days but she couldn't imagine what her aunt and uncle would need anything too sophisticated for. There was no password. She wasn't surprised. In a town where people rarely, if ever, locked their doors, they wouldn't see the need for password protecting their computer. Much to her surprise, the battery still had a charge and she wondered if the staff at Graceful Acres had something to do with it.

The system itself was old and it took a while to boot up. Addison drummed her finger on the base as she waited.

"Okay, let's see here. What am I looking for...e-mail?" Someone must've helped set this up because there was an e-mail icon on the desktop. Easy-peasy. Well, once she created a hotspot using her cell phone. "Found it."

She checked the inbox just in case. She highly doubted her aunt and cousin were in contact via e-mail, but it was worth a shot. She skimmed all the ads and the occasional name, clicking on anything that wasn't a bot. "Nothing so far."

The sound of a vehicle heading their way stopped her search. Plus, she was doing this the hard way. She put Ivy's name in the search bar. Got four hits. "I got something."

"Stay with it, I'll talk to the sheriff." He exited the truck as the marked SUV pulled up beside them and parked.

Fingers on the ready, she clicked the one of the bottom of the list, the oldest one. The date coincided with the time period her parents had called Addison's mother to see if their daughter had run away there. That wasn't the question that had been asked at the time and she couldn't remember the date exactly, only the year that coincided with Ivy turning seventeen and Addison being sixteen. They'd asked if Addison had seen her cousin. Looking back, that's not what they had meant. They wanted to know if Ivy was at Addison's house or if she knew of her cousin's plans to run away. Her heart went out to them for the pain they must've felt at realizing their teenage daughter hadn't come home. The horror that would come with those feelings. It had to be every parent's worst nightmare aside from a child dying. It some ways, this must have been just as difficult. The not knowing what had happened would be knives to the chest.

The subject line on the oldest e-mail read, *help!* There were dozens of scams with the same subject line. Was that the reason her e-mail had been filtered? Once her name had been marked, the other e-mails would receive the same fate.

Reading the body of the note was a gut punch.

*I'm sorry. I was stupid. I made a mistake. Please send money so I can come home.* There was an address, which Addison immediately looked up. It was a gas station east of Austin.

Why not call? Why send an e-mail?

The obvious answer was that she didn't have access to a phone. The possibility she was being held against her will in an unfamiliar area sank in. When no money came, she must have thought her parents turned their backs on her.

The next e-mail was dated roughly eight months later.

*I want to come home.*

Reading those five words brought tears to Addison's eyes. She quickly clicked on the next one dated three weeks later.

*Everything is fine. I was playing a prank before. I'm good.*

And then the final one that had Ivy as the subject line but came from a different e-mail address.

*He's going to kill me.*

Addison waved the sheriff over, trying to shake off the sudden chill racing down her spine while thinking how sad it was that Ivy's parents never received her cries for help as all the messages were previously unread. She had so many questions as she opened the passenger door and turned the screen for the sheriff to see. "These messages are from my cousin to her parents. Based on the fact there were no replies and the messages were highlighted in bold, my guess is they never saw them."

Sheriff Justice skimmed the opened message before clicking a few keys to read the others. Her face carried the stress of her job, stress lines bracketing her mouth, worry lines etched into her forehead. She was still a stunning woman to be sure. It was clear she cared deeply about the people in her county.

"A simple investigation when the Murrays first complained might have made a difference," the sheriff said.

"She obviously never turned up here, unless she returned and is responsible for the break-ins," Addison pointed out.

"Do you mind me asking how much you stand to inherit?"

"It's not much. In fact, I'll be lucky to break even if I can get this place ready and on the market in a couple of weeks. The sooner, the better since my business back home will start suffering if I'm away for too long."

"And you have no idea if there were any valuables in the home?"

"None. I can't imagine why a person would be breaking in now that my aunt and uncle are gone. I mean, the first break-in could have happened a while ago for all we know. But this one...obviously not the case."

"The perp has to be watching the house," the sheriff said, the worry lines deepening.

Didn't that send another icy chill racing down Addison's back?

～

THE NEW INFORMATION on Ivy was a game-changer. Reed kept his eye on the surrounding trees, scanning the landscape for a place someone could easily camp and watch the house without getting caught. Nighttime would be easy considering there were no outside lights here. He remembered seeing a light over the door of the barn but neither him or Addison had turned it on once in the time they'd been staying here.

A rustling in the underbrush to the east of the house caught his attention. "Hold on."

He took off toward the commotion. More scrub brush moved as he stared down the area. There could be a wild animal causing the disturbance or it was possible he was about the catch a peeper red-handed. Either way, he'd know what he was dealing with in a few seconds. He also realized he wasn't doing near enough cardio because halfway across the lawn, he was already winded. His thigh burned too.

Pushing faster, he doubled his pace ignoring his screaming calves. Whatever was making the noise in front of him seemed ready and able to pick up the pace too, so he wasn't gaining any ground.

At the end of the yard where trees and scrub brush separated this from the neighbor's property, Reed stopped. He was breathing hard and he put a hand on his side where it ached as he scoured the trees. Going in could be a mistake. The trees were dense and the scrub brush would make traversing the terrain difficult. He could end up alone in there without his pistol, which he'd tucked underneath his seat when the sheriff arrived. He had a conceal and carry license, so he wasn't doing anything wrong. But he figured it would be best to keep his weapon out of view as he exited the vehicle on her arrival.

He couldn't see any movement. Whatever was in there was long gone by now. He looked around to get a sense of what it might have been. Probably a scared squirrel or raccoon.

Not ready to admit defeat, he walked the perimeter. As he neared the barn, he saw a break in the scrub brush just behind the tree line. There was an impression on the ground and the area looked like it had been cleared as though someone had set up camp.

Taking a step inside, he saw a discarded water bottle and a wadded up fast food napkin. He jogged back to the vehicles and updated the sheriff on his findings. She followed him to the spot after a quick stop to grab a couple of evidence bags. At the tree line, she paused long enough to put on a pair of gloves before collecting evidence.

"The theory someone has been watching the house is seeming more likely than before," she said.

"Why? Are they looking for something?" He wanted to hear the sheriff's perspective.

"Seems like a good reason. They are either looking for something or sneaking small things out. Things that we might not notice."

"The place was dusty, but we spent some time yesterday cleaning it up. Might be harder to figure out what this person is looking for." He shook his head. "This has to be her cousin, right?"

"Who knows? The cousin is as good a guess as any," she said. "The break-ins started after their deaths. So, it's anyone's guess. Where were the Murrays living?"

"Graceful Acres off farm road 237."

"I'll swing by and interview the staff there. See if they had any visitors. It wouldn't hurt to ask how well the staff knew them."

"There's a sweet maintenance guy there by the name of Elton. He took good care of the laptop and phone. He seemed to know how important the quilted carrying bag was to Mrs. Murray."

Sheriff Justice's eyebrow went up. "Do you have a last name for him?"

"No." He shook his head for emphasis. "I only saw his name because it had been stitched into his shirt. He seemed like he knew the older couple."

"What about people who might know about Addison's inheritance?" Sheriff Justice asked.

"She's having a dust up with her mother's new husband. I don't get the impression there's any love lost between the two of them. In fact, he seems to be making her life hell. Logistically, he's in Dallas, so I doubt he's the one breaking in," he said.

"I'd still like to speak to him," she said. "From all appearances, Ivy got herself involved with an abusive relationship."

"No real man ever hits anyone smaller or weaker than him." His hands fisted thinking about it.

"Agreed. Young people make mistakes and sometimes get mixed up with the wrong people."

"I doubt anyone has a spotless record when it comes to judging others, especially when young, inexperienced hormones are involved. What feels like love in the moment turns out to be infatuation. Of course, the person in it doesn't realize it until much later. Usually when they're old enough to experience real love for the first time." Reed had to say that while he'd dated around enough to know when he met someone special, Addison fit the bill of everything he would want in a partner, intelligent, strong, independent, sense of humor. On top of those qualities, she was just about the most beautiful person he'd ever set eyes on. Not that he was biased, but she was the complete package.

"We've all made a mistake or two in the love department. Experience is the best teacher," she agreed.

Reed looked at Addison, who was sitting in his truck, looking like she belonged there, and his heart clenched.

Could he keep her safe if someone was after something at the Murray house? The break-ins were escalating. Did that mean someone was becoming desperate? Would that person be willing to hurt her if she got in the way?

15

By the time Reed returned with the sheriff, Addison needed to stretch her legs outside of the truck. She couldn't go inside the house for fear she would trample evidence. All she could do was stand outside and try to keep the blood moving.

"Anything else on the computer we should know about?" Reed asked as he neared.

"I didn't find anything to be concerned about."

"How well do you know the employees at Graceful Acres?" Sheriff Justice asked.

"Not very well. I just met them after learning my aunt had passed away. My aunt didn't want a funeral. She had all the arrangements spelled out. I was to be notified after her cremation. She didn't want me to be sad. So, five days is all. Why?" She sucked in a breath as she realized the implication. "You don't think..."

"I need to follow up on all possibilities."

Did that mean the sheriff believed Ivy was out of the picture? Permanently? A heavy blanket of dread covered

Addison's shoulders as the sheriff excused herself to collect evidence and investigate the home break-in.

Once she concluded her initial survey, she returned to the porch. "Would you mind coming inside to see if any of your belongings are missing?"

Addison obliged with Hero not far behind her. She was getting on with the dog better than she expected in a short time. Did he know on instinct how far she would go in order to protect him? He was still timid, don't get her wrong. But at least he wasn't shying away from her now.

The main thing she'd brought into the house of value was her laptop. So, she headed to the kitchen and where she remembered leaving it on the table. There it was. "Huh."

"What's wrong?" Reed asked. She looked up at him only to realize he was studying her.

"I could have sworn I closed my laptop. I mean, it's normally my habit. But it's open and I don't remember leaving it that way." She was off her norm, though, so that didn't prove anything.

"Mind if I dust for prints?" Sheriff Justice asked.

"Be my guest." It was probably just her mind playing tricks on her. Why would someone break into the house and not steal her laptop? Why would they leave it open? She was probably just remembering wrong. Everything in her life was being turned upside-down and she wasn't thinking clearly. There was a simple explanation.

The sheriff went to work.

"At this rate, I'll never get this place ready for sale," she said to Reed.

He turned and walked over to the coffee maker. "Do you want a fresh cup?"

She couldn't read his tone but there was a note in his voice that gave her pause. Offended?

"Yes, please. I can help."

"I got it," he said.

The sheriff finished up dusting the laptop and then excused herself promising to report back her findings if she got anything this time.

"The sheriff mentioned interviewing the care facility employees. Think there's anything to it?" She'd almost lost hope on finding Ivy. Once she settled up this house and her aunt and uncle's affairs, she would go back to her full-time life. Suddenly, the prospect felt like a prison sentence.

"A fresh cup of coffee." He held up the brew and she could already smell how amazing it was going to taste.

"Thank you." She took a sip and practically groaned with pleasure.

He shot another look at her she didn't dare question. This look, she understood. No explanation needed. And she wanted the same thing—to see how much better the dark roast would taste on his lips. Giving into the chemistry pinging between them wouldn't make her think any more clearly. It would be an amazing distraction. She couldn't argue there.

"Is it crazy to want the break-ins to be my cousin?"

"Why wouldn't she just show her face at this point?" His question struck a nerve. He was right. She had no reason to hide. Or did she?

"Maybe she's still with that guy." It was a logical assumption. Right?

"After all this time?" he asked.

"It's possible."

"I wouldn't bet on it. She was trying to get out years ago," he pointed out.

"The messages stopped."

"Maybe because your aunt and uncle never responded." Again, it was logical.

"It's possible she believed they'd written her off. There was so much despair in her messages. They never knew their own daughter wanted to come home."

"He might have threatened to harm her parents if she ever left him," he said.

"And she would have believed him." Oh, man, was her heart aching for this sweet family who, by all accounts, disconnected over a misunderstanding.

"From everything I've seen or heard of victims of abuse, they believe their abuser's threats."

Addison shook her head, wishing it wasn't true for her cousin. "It's just so hard to believe Ivy would fall into that trap."

"After the last e-mail, it doesn't seem like she ever tried to reach her parents again. I gave the sheriff the phone when we were outside. She can analyze the numbers."

"It's a cold case, my cousin. It's a cold trail that seems to have ended with the e-mails."

"Let's put ourselves in her shoes for a second. Why come back now? And if she did, why break-in. If she's alive, she could challenge the will. It happens all the time."

"She might have read the obituary."

"If they're gone, the guy she was with would haven't have a hold over her."

"True." Addison blew out a frustrated breath.

THE EVIDENCE WASN'T POINTING to Ivy. It didn't add up to Reed. If she was with someone who kept her under his thumb all these years by threatening to hurt her parents, why not come forward now that they were dead?

Why sneak in the back door and then break in the front? His first thought was that she might be looking for some type of will, but why not go to the sheriff and stake a claim?

He set thoughts of Ivy aside. After the last e-mail, he feared the worst might have happened to her. "The sheriff is right about the facility. Now that I think about it, they were with your aunt and uncle twenty-four-seven. What if your aunt let it slip that she had valuables here in the house?"

"That's possible. They were definitely the hide-money-under-the-mattress types." She got a spark in her eye before glancing upstairs.

"It's worth a shot." He followed closely behind her as she made quick work of the staircase. She cut left to the master bedroom and then dropped onto her knees in front of the bed. She gave him a look of hope before running her hands in between the mattress and boxed spring.

"I feel something." She pulled out money, just as they'd suspected.

"Let me move this whole thing." He put a hand on either side of bed, spreading his arms, and then shoved the mattress off the boxed spring.

"There's something here all right." Addison produced a wooden, hand-carved box.

"This might just be what our intruder is looking for."

She sat down on the floor and crisscrossed her legs. "There's no lock."

"Who would think that someone would literally hide valuables under the mattress in this day and age?"

"I know. It boggles the mind. It's too simple." She opened the lid to reveal several gold pieces, mostly rings and necklaces. She picked them up and examined them. "These are eighteen karat gold."

"Definitely worth something," he said.

"They must be family heirlooms. This one," she pulled out a solid gold pocket watch, "could be worth a lot. It looks like an antique."

"This could be what our intruder is looking for."

"My mind keeps snapping to Ivy. But it's possible I just want it to be her, so I know she's safe."

"I better let the sheriff know what we've found."

Before he could pull his phone out of his pocket, it buzzed. He fished it out and checked the screen. "Speak of the devil."

Reed answered the call.

"Do you want to hear the good news or the bad news first?" the sheriff asked.

"Mind if I put this call on speaker?"

"Not a bit," she said.

"Okay." He did. "Addison is here with me."

After perfunctory greetings, she continued, "Good news or bad?"

"Bad news," Addison said without hesitation.

"Still no prints. Whoever is doing this is careful not to leave a trail," she said.

"Career criminal?" Reed asked.

"Not necessarily. Could be someone who watches crime shows on TV or has internet access. You can learn pretty much anything on the internet," she said.

Reed knew this was true from personal experience after he learned in twenty-four hours how to cook a turkey when Miss Penny was down with a bad cold one Thanksgiving. The cooking site told him what to do and Thanksgiving dinner had been saved. Win-win.

"And the good news?" Addison asked.

"Well, this is really good news for you, Addison." The sheriff paused a few seconds. "I tracked down Ivy. She's alive and has a five-year-old daughter. She changed her name and that's why she was presumed dead. She's living in Montana now and I have confirmation it's her. She's a waitress at a Sundown Café and a single mom."

The biggest smile Reed have ever seen covered Addison's face. "She's alive?"

"That's right. According to her boss, she's the most responsible waitress he's ever had work for him. She dotes on her daughter and is obsessed with the little girl."

"Have you spoken to her?" A rogue tear ran down Addison's cheek. Reed thumbed it away.

"I have. She sounded good. I informed her about her parents."

"And?" Addison's question came quickly.

"She wants to speak to you. I have a phone number if you'd like to reach out to her."

"I'd like that very much, actually."

"Good. I'll send it via text. I think you'll understand what's going on better once you speak to her. But she's in Montana and has been, so she's not responsible for the break-ins," the sheriff said.

"Then, who is?" she asked.

"They're still under investigation."

"Have you spoken to the staff at Graceful Acres?" Reed interjected.

"That's in process." She paused. "I promise to report back as soon as I know anything."

"We have news on our side," Addison continued.

"Oh?"

"We found a box full of what look like family heirlooms," Addison reported. "I couldn't begin to assess the value but I'm staring an antique pocket watch as well as a lot of pure gold pieces."

"That's interesting." Laney's tone changed to curious.

"It might be what our person is looking for," Addison noted.

"Can you take a picture? Also, log the contents. You might want to think about keeping them somewhere other than the house, especially after what happened to the front door."

"I want to leave even less. Seems like every time we do, there's another break in," she said.

"True. My question would be whether or not it's safe to be there with valuables. On the other hand, the intruder only breaks in when you guys are gone. You slept there last night and everything was fine."

"I can have one of my brothers or cousins pick up the valuables," Reed chimed in. "It's a good idea to keep them off property for a while until this is all settled."

"That sounds like the best option," she said to Reed.

He ended the call with the sheriff after saying goodbyes and then texted Levi. The response was immediate.

*On my way.*

Reed would have to dig into his bag of tricks in order to repair the front door. For the time being, he might board it up and then have someone come out to replace it.

The second text that came through was from the sheriff. It was Ivy's phone number.

He held the screen toward Addison. "Ready to make a call?"

She stared at it for a long moment.

"Not yet."

He must've shot a look because she quickly added, "I will. I just need time."

"You might want to contact the estate lawyer and ask how this changes things for your inheritance."

"I was just about to go over my list of things to take care of to prep the house for sale. I was thinking that I needed a recommendation for a Realtor." A look of relief crossed her features. "If this house should belong to my cousin and not me, that certainly changes my to-do list and how long I need to be here." She tangled her fingers together. "I might be free from this place and back home sooner than I thought."

The thought knotted his gut. It shouldn't. He shouldn't allow it to take hold. Except the thought of her walking away and him going back to his usual routine left a hollow feeling in his chest.

16

The minute Addison spoke the words out loud, an unsettled feeling came over her. Going back to Dallas—why did that suddenly feel so...*empty*?

The feeling encompassed more than just the moment, but she chalked it up to being overtired and overwrought in her emotions. Did she want Reed on a primal level? The answer was a quick yes, and a hell, yeah.

A physical relationship might satisfy the moment but the aftershocks could be devastating when she walked away. The business needed her. Her employees needed her. Her mother needed her.

Suddenly, the reasons for going home didn't hold as much power over her. The draw to care for a business she stepped into and ran successfully wasn't as strong a pull as it used to be. The idea of caring for her mother despite the woman making the decision to marry someone Addison didn't like or trust felt like an unnecessary burden. And the way she put her own hopes and dreams on hold as they were just beginning to take shape struck her as unfair for the first time. After losing her father, there'd been no time for questions. She'd jumped into action and done a helluva job. Her mother wasn't making it easy. In fact, she seemed more dependent than ever. Also, the demands she was starting to make along with her husband weren't sitting right either.

And why wasn't her mother taking her side for a change? Why was she allowing a guy she'd married a couple of months ago who she'd known less than a year step in and take over?

She pushed up to standing. "My phone is downstairs and so is my laptop." She was still trying to figure out why a fortune hunter wouldn't at least grab her expensive computer. The person seemed to be going after a specific thing and not just anything available. Had the intruder even gone into the kitchen? It was possible he or she didn't know the laptop was in there. After trying the laundry room, the person might have moved their search elsewhere. The perp seemed to be targeting a specific area of the house for the search.

*Someone with inside knowledge.*

It had to be someone with intimate knowledge of her aunt and uncle. Her mind snapped to the facility. Were there nurses or caregivers who got close enough to get the information out of her aunt or uncle? Did someone over-hear a conversation? Since her aunt and uncle were gone, it was impossible to ask them.

Addison set those thoughts aside as she made her way downstairs. Hero curled up on his bed in the living room as she passed through. She couldn't help but think how comfortable he looked. Going back to her old life so soon would leave less time to nurse him back to health.

Her laptop sat on the kitchen table, just as she'd left it. She opened it and powered up. A minute or so later and she pulled up her e-mail. She located the last e-mail from the lawyer and then typed a response.

*Is there a provision for my cousin if she is living?*

Addison's heart broke at the pain Ivy had obviously endured being in an abusive relationship. But that was years ago. Why hadn't she tried to contact her parents after that last haunting e-mail? Why had the attempt at communication stopped? And for this many years? Ivy had to know her parents were aging. She also had to realize they wouldn't be around forever. What made her cut off all contact?

As frustrating as Addison's mother could be—and believe her when she said the woman could work Addison's last nerve—there was never a time when she would cut her out of her life completely. Not if her mother wanted to have a relationship. Addison didn't have to like the person her mother chose to marry, but she would be there to support her mother in the best way she could no matter what else happened.

So, making the call to Ivy was daunting. Would Addison be speaking to a stranger now? Nothing about the person she knew added up with what Ivy had become.

Ivy was a mother now. A mother. She worked as a waitress when all she'd ever talked about was finding a way to make a living doing crafts or commercial art. She spent her time doodling and crafting. For instance, the way she'd added a beautiful pattern on her dresser during her mod podge phase. Addison had never been much of a crafter, but she always loved helping Ivy.

Of course, if she could own any business, she would have opened a sweet shop. Nothing too big. She would have saved her money and gone someplace fancy like Paris instead of college to study confection. Or maybe Belgium to learn everything she could about chocolate.

Her phone alerted her to an incoming e-mail from the lawyer.

*It could make the will contestable in court. It would be up to their heir to challenge it.*

Addison didn't necessarily want the responsibility of selling her aunt and uncle's place but she cared a lot about carrying out their final wishes. She wanted to honor their memories in the best way that she could.

"Can you grab a two-by-four from the barn?" Reed called out from the living room.

"No problem." She closed her laptop, needing a minute to think as she walked outside. At the door, she gave a backward glance at Hero to find him sleeping in his bed. Rather than disturb him, she exited through the back of the house.

A two-by-four. She walked the half a football field from the house to the barn. There were spiderwebs everywhere along with broken and rotted boards. Creepy. The barn wasn't scary back when it was kept up to date, had a horse and pony in the stalls and goats running around. There were chickens. The coop was behind the barn and toward the back of the lawn.

It was daylight outside, midday at this point. Her stomach reminded her of how little she'd eaten so far today.

The barn door creaked as she opened it. Inside was dark as night, save for the slivers of sunlight creeping in through the cracks. It had an eerie, haunted feeling as she slipped inside. Her grip tightened on the cell phone in her hand as she thumbed around to get the flashlight app going.

Just as part of the room was bathed in light, she heard a familiar-sounding male voice that sent a shiver racing down her spine.

Then, everything went black.

REED WHISTLED WHILE HE WORKED. It was a habit he'd picked up as a kid and had never quite gotten rid of. He glanced toward the kitchen. Addison had acknowledged his request. She'd gone. Right?

He moved into the room. Empty. From the back window, he saw a male figure carrying her over his shoulder. Her limbs hung like a ragdoll's.

Reed mumbled a curse and tore off through the kitchen door. He pushed his legs hard. The male figure cursed and turned toward the trees. Reed had an advantage since he wasn't carrying more than a hundred pounds of dead weight.

As he crossed the halfway mark of the yard, the perp threw Addison's limp body toward Reed and then bolted toward the trees. He was wearing all black; joggers and a cotton shirt. He had on a baseball cap, pulled low on his brow. The hat was black but from this distance, Reed couldn't see the man's hair color.

Addison bounced as she hit the ground hard. He immediately dovetailed toward her and dropped down to his knees. There was fresh blood in her hair and on her face. He quickly scanned her, looking for the source. She'd been struck with something on the back of her head. There was a gash. Reed checked her pulse and got one. He repositioned her head and neck to ease any strain from the awkward landing. She'd rolled a couple of times and that most likely helped absorb the fall.

A whoosh of air, a blur of black fur, and Hero blew past Reed at an incredible pace.

The sound of Levi's voice in the background was all Reed needed as he hopped to his feet and took off toward the perp. Enough. This person had gone too far and Reed had no plans to let him get away with it.

Heart in his throat, worry eating at him from the inside out, Reed followed behind Hero. He'd lost sight of the perp in the thick mesquites and even thicker undergrowth. He had to hop through it as much as try to run.

It slowed down the perp too because Hero started barking and then things went dead quiet for a second before a male voice cut through the thicket. The half-growl, half-shout sounded a few seconds before the word, "Help."

By the time Reed caught up, the perp was on the ground and Hero was on top of him, showing his teeth and growling in a manner so fierce that Reed was taken back. The Lab's protective instincts must've kicked in and the sight warmed Reed's heart.

"Good boy, Hero." Reed approached as the perp rolled like an alligator with prey in its mouth.

Caught off balance, Hero yelped as he was thrown off balance. Reed didn't miss a beat. As soon as the animal was cleared from the perp, Reed dove on top of the man. He contained the perp with his heft and then squeezed his thighs until the perp couldn't move his bottom half. The man was strong, though, and threw a punch that threatened to reset Reed's clock. The fist landed on his left jaw and caused his head to snap in that direction. The impact knocked spit out of his mouth.

Hero was bearing down again, firing off barks.

Reed reared back and slammed his fist into the blue-eyed perp's cheekbone. The impact caused Blue-eyes to lose focus before his eyelids came down, out cold.

"Good boy, Hero." Reed repositioned to make certain the perp couldn't budge if he woke.

Not a minute later, Levi was there.

"I'll take over here. Go to her," Levi said. Since his cousin was as powerful as Reed, if not more so despite the fact Reed would never admit that to Levi's face, he got up and let his cousin take over. "Sheriff is on her way. I can sit on this jerk until she gets here."

With a quick *thank you*, Reed was off and Hero was by his side. The dog had a limp but it didn't seem like there was any way he would stay with Levi.

As Reed cleared the trees and got his first look at Addison sitting up, his heart unclenched for the first time since he saw the perp running with her.

She looked up and her expression morphed the minute she locked eyes with Reed. He charged to her side and dropped down next to her, afraid to touch her. She threw her arms around him and he gently wrapped his arms around her.

"It was my mother's husband, Reed. Why would he do that?"

"Jesus, I thought I lost you," he said in the only response he could. The weight of those words struck him full force because there was no way he wanted to live without her again. He couldn't go back to that dark, hollow existence ever again. Addison was the light and he wanted to grab hold and hang onto it, to her. He dropped his gaze and said, "I can't lose you."

"I'm in trouble, Reed," she said as they embraced.

"Where are you hurt?"

"No. Not that kind. My heart. It sounds crazy because we've only spent a couple of days together, but when you know, you just know. I've fallen hard for you and Dallas no longer feels like home. Although I love this place, it never felt like my home. The only place I feel home is when I'm with you. I think I've fallen in love with you."

He feathered kisses up her neck until he found her mouth and pressed his lips to hers gently. When he pulled back, he said, "I'm head over heels for you, Addison. I love you and I don't ever want to be apart again. I'll take whatever you can give me but understand that, when you're ready, I intend to ask you to be my wife."

"I don't need to wait to say the word, yes. My heart is all-in with you, Reed McGannon. All except for the part that belongs to this guy. My other guy, Hero. As long as your proposal includes this guy, I have no problem saying yes. He deserves a forever home as much as I do."

Hero was there, by their side, and Reed had every intention of making that arrangement permanent too. He was the perfect companion for them to start their family.

"He tunneled his way into my heart the moment I saw him. No family of ours would be complete with our Hero."

17

"I f you bring me coffee in bed one more day, I might never leave this room." Addison teased her new fiancé.

"Good thing I plan to marry you before the head injury wears off and you change your mind," he teased.

Was he kidding? She counted herself as the luckiest person in the world to have found the kind of love she knew in her heart would last.

"I'm pretty certain you're the one who leapt before he looked," she teased right back, taking the fresh cup of coffee. She took a sip and mewled. "Did I hear voices downstairs or was that the TV?"

"No TV."

She had insisted on staying at her aunt and uncle's place since this was where Hero had everything set up. Besides, she wanted to be in full form when she and Reed moved into their home on the ranch.

"Was it the sheriff?"

"Nope. But you're right about hearing voices. Two. Females." He stood up and backed toward the door, blocking her view. And then he stepped aside.

"Ivy?" Her tears welled as she took a look at her cousin with a beautiful, curly-haired five-year-old girl.

"I hope it's okay that we came." Ivy stood there, holding her daughter's hand. The shy girl practically hid behind her mother's leg. She had the biggest brown eyes and most adorable round face.

"Okay if I leave you guys alone?" Reed asked.

"Yes. Of course."

He walked over to the bed, leaned forward and kissed her. "I love you."

"Love you too."

"I'll be downstairs if you need me. Hollar." He winked at her and that caused a dozen butterflies to release in her chest and her stomach to freefall.

"We'll be fine."

He disappeared down the hall and Ivy took another tentative step forward.

"Do you want to sit down?" Addison asked.

"Sure." Her cousin looked so mature now.

"You have a beautiful daughter," Addison said.

Ivy practically beamed. She set her daughter up on the floor with a coloring book and crayons on the rug next to the window.

Then, just like they were kids again, Ivy kicked off her shoes and climbed in bed beside Addison.

"I hear you just got engaged." She motioned toward the gold band on Addison's ring finger.

"He's too special to let walk out of my life."

"And it's Reed McGannon." Ivy's cheeks blushed.

"He's pretty much everything I could ever want in a man."

"And still hot."

They laughed.

And then Addison took a sip of coffee. She needed to ask the question that had been on her mind since finding out the news of the inheritance. "Why did you leave, Ivy?"

"A guy." She glanced over at her daughter. "The wrong one. Took me a while to figure that out and then even longer to get out from under his thumb."

"Why didn't you come back? I mean, I know how much your parents loved you."

Tears streamed down Ivy's face. "I sent them e-mails and they never responded. I wanted to hear from them so badly it..."

She glanced over at her daughter again as she quickly wiped away the evidence of her sadness. It was heavy and Addison could feel it rolling off Ivy in waves.

"They never got them, Ivy. Your e-mails went straight into Spam. I'm guessing the subject line caused them to get caught in the spam filter. Your parents never knew you were trying to reach them, Ivy. They would have given their right arms to help you. You know that, right?"

More of those tears leaked out of her eyes. "I thought they hated me after I hurt them. Teenagers can do some pretty stupid things."

"Your parents would never hate you. Ever. They had nothing but love for you."

"I let him convince me that I was unlovable. That I was bad. It took getting away from him to wake up and realize what he'd been doing to me," she admitted. "Her dad was different. He loved me. He loved her so much."

Addison reached out and pulled Ivy into a hug.

"Where is he now?" She didn't see a ring on Ivy's finger, not that it always worked out that marriage came before a baby.

"He was killed in a motorcycle crash around her first

birthday. We had all these plans. He was working two jobs so I could be with her full-time. I was planning to start online classes for art."

"I'm so sorry, Ivy." She just held her cousin. The person who had suffered so much heartache and deserved another chance, a better chance.

"I've missed you so much," she said.

"Me too, honey."

Ivy pulled back and gathered herself with another quick glance at her daughter.

"What do you think about coming home?" Addison asked. "Your parents left this place to me because they honestly believed you were..."

Ivy nodded and took in a deep breath.

"I couldn't. I wouldn't even be able to afford to keep up the place."

"What if I told you that your parents had a secret stash worth more than enough money to put you through art school while she's in kindergarten?"

"I'd pinch myself because I would have to be dreaming."

"It's true, Ivy. They would want you to have all this. It's your legacy, not mine. They just didn't know how to reach you."

"I would love to have a real home again. I can feel them when I'm here. You know?"

Addison was already nodding before Ivy finished her sentence.

"Plus, I'm moving to Cattle Cove and I need my family here."

"What about your mom? Where is she?"

"She's staying in Dallas to run the deli. She seems to be stepping up after marrying a disaster of a man who tried to kill me for this inheritance." The original break-ins had

been Elton. He was in financial trouble and he'd managed
to swindle a couple of the old people in the home. Now, he
was behind bars where he belonged. She hoped him and
Benjamin could share a cell. But she had no plans to dwell
on it.

They were locked behind bars. Her mother was finally
stepping up to take charge of her own life after that wake-up
call. And Addison was starting a new life with her soon-to-
be husband.

Plus, she had a second cousin to get to know.

"What's her name?" Addison asked.

"Kay. After my mom," Ivy beamed.

"Mommy?" the little girl's sweet little voice asked.

"Yes, baby?"

"Who is that?" she whispered like Addison somehow
wouldn't be able to hear.

"That's your Aunt Addison."

"I have an aunt?"

"Yes, baby. You do now."

REED MADE sure he didn't have anything metal on him as he
walked toward the justice center. There was nothing that
could be used as a weapon. He brought only a thin wallet
and his keys, which he handed over to the officer at the
entrance.

After being patted down, he was asked a series of questions. He gave his name and told them who he wanted
to see.

He hadn't been this unsettled since he first heard the
news of his father's arrest. It was time to clear the air, he

thought, as he was led down a corridor and into a room that looked a lot like a gray-colored school cafeteria.

Reed was instructed to sit at table number three, which he did. He watched as his father was led into the room. His handcuffs were removed and then he was walked over to the table. In the weeks since he'd been here, he looked like he'd aged five years.

"Hello, son," Donny McGannon said.

"Father."

"It's good to see you."

"Sorry I haven't been by before now."

"No child should have to see his father locked up like an animal."

"I'm not a child." Reed studied his father. Guilty or innocent? He searched his father's eyes, looking deep, trying to find the answer.

"No. I didn't mean to offend you. I'm glad you came."

Reed put his hands on the table and clasped his fingers. "How are you?"

"I'm okay," he said. "I've had a lot of time to think in here, Reed. I have a confession to make."

All of Reed's muscles tensed. "Okay."

"I've been a lousy father."

Reed didn't have a response to that. He couldn't argue. Although, he might add absent father to the list.

"I have a lot of regrets in life," he continued. "But I didn't try to kill my brother."

18

EPILOGUE

Hayden McGannon was in a mood.

His Uncle Clive had remembered arguing with his brother, Hayden's dad. In fact, it seemed to be the last thing he remembered before taking a 'fall' that cost him weeks on end in the hospital with doctors unsure if he would make a meaningful recovery.

Thank the heavens Uncle Clive was going to be fine. Better than fine. He was topnotch and returning to his normal self with each passing day. Hayden couldn't go to the equipment room with the group earlier. He just couldn't.

Did that make him a jerk? Maybe.

But he loved McGannon Herd. He loved the land. He loved his family, except for the sperm donor he barely knew. Hayden was keeping his father at arm's length before the arrest. Now? He was definitely steering clear. There was no way he wanted to be caught in the middle between the man who'd raised him like his own and the one who genetically was his dad.

It took a helluva lot more than sex to make someone a father. Fathers stuck around through the hard times. Fathers showed up when they were needed. Fathers were the model for a growing boy to look up to. They didn't cash in their inheritance and bolt without a backward glance. They didn't leave their five young sons with no explanation or forewarning. They sure as hell didn't disappear for years on end and only return when they were broke, asking for a handout.

Hayden had volunteered to run fences as far away from the main house as he could get today. So, it surprised him when his cell buzzed in his pocket. He must have been standing in just the right place because coverage was almost non-existent this far out.

Wasn't that just his luck?

"Hey, Reed. What's up?" A sinking feeling hit in the pit of his stomach as he took the call.

"Just calling to see if you've heard the news." His brother's voice was unreadable. He must be calling about what happened in the equipment room.

"No. What's the word?" he asked, not sure if he really wanted to know the truth. A piece of him wanted his father to be innocent. Hayden didn't want to believe his father was capable of attempted murder, especially with family.

"Brant and Cage are moving." Reed's news couldn't be further from what Hayden was expecting. Wasn't this supposed to be an update about their father?

"Hold on a minute. I need a repeat on that because I must not have heard right the first time," Hayden said.

Reed said it again.

"Where to? And why?" More questions hit but these felt like the two most important ones.

"They said they'd let us know once they figured it out. They've been looking at Colorado," Reed supplied.

"Did you know any of this?" The family had lived and

worked side-by-side on the ranch Hayden's entire life. Theirs too.

"I literally just found out fifteen minutes ago."

"Were they planning on having a meeting to talk this through?" Hayden was in shock. He'd never once heard either of his brothers mention a move.

"They said no meeting. In fact, they stayed up all night last night once the idea struck. Said they'd talked about it before but never seriously."

"What do they plan to do once they get to Colorado or wherever they're going?" Hayden's heart ached and he wasn't covering his emotions very well despite being good at doing just that most of the time. It was the extreme nature of the situation with their uncle and father. And now this?

"Taco stand."

Hayden took a minute to let that sink in.

"Said they have plenty of money to get by considering all they ever do is bank their checks."

There was no reason to spend money, considering basically every need was fulfilled at the ranch. They all had their own homes. Miss Penny kept them all stocked with food. They only thing they ever needed to buy was a vehicle and most kept the same one for as long as it drove.

Hayden issued a sharp sigh. The world had been changing around him and he felt like he was on one of those merry-go-rounds, standing in the middle, watching as everything spun around him. It had been this way ever since the accident.

"You know Brant better than anyone. Any chance they'll change their minds?" Hayden hated the family splitting up.

"I seriously doubt it. It was the most excited I'd seen him about anything in a long time," Reed admitted.

When he really thought about it, he wouldn't want them to stick around and be miserable.

"Said he has a need to prove himself and so does Cage." Those two had always been close. And, yes, they could make a mean taco. "They want to make something successful from the ground up."

That, Hayden understood. Ranching was in his blood and he loved the land. But being at McGannon Herd was losing its appeal with everything going on. The place where he'd grown up and called home seemed different lately. Empty?

Nah, he shook off the thought. The ranch was home and he wasn't missing anything in his life.

To READ Mika and Hayden's story, click here.

# ALSO BY BARB HAN

**Cowboys of Cattle Cove**

Cowboy Reckoning

Cowboy Cover-up

Cowboy Retribution

Cowboy Judgment

Cowboy Conspiracy

Cowboy Rescue

Cowboy Target

Cowboy Redemption

Cowboy Intrigue

Cowboy Ransom

**Don't Mess With Texas Cowboys**

Texas Cowboy's Protection (*FREE*)

Texas Cowboy Justice

Texas Cowboy's Honor

Texas Cowboy Daddy

Texas Cowboy's Baby

Texas Cowboy's Bride

Texas Cowboy's Family

**Crisis: Cattle Barge**

Sudden Setup

Endangered Heiress

Texas Grit

Kidnapped at Christmas

Murder and Mistletoe

Bulletproof Christmas

For more of Barb's books, visit www.BarbHan.com.

## ABOUT THE AUTHOR

Barb Han is a USA TODAY and Publisher's Weekly Best-selling Author. Reviewers have called her books "heartfelt" and "exciting."

Barb lives in Texas—her true north—with her adventurous family, a poodle mix and a spunky rescue who is often referred to as a hot mess. She is the proud owner of too many books (if there is such a thing). When not writing, she can be found exploring Manhattan, on a mountain either hiking or skiing depending on the season, or swimming in her own backyard.

Sign up for Barb's newsletter at www.BarbHan.com.